Praise for *Down to Earth*

"A steamy modern romance for the ages: This is for anyone who finds sexual tension in the produce aisle, who fantasizes about a country love affair, who loves clever, tender writing, flirting, and farming."

—Alison Roman, *New York Times* bestselling author

"I gobbled this up. *Down to Earth* made me laugh, swoon, and smile hard at the end. I can't wait for more fiction from Julia Turshen."

—Jasmine Guillory, *New York Times* bestselling author of *Flirting Lessons*

Down to Earth

JULIA TURSHEN

831 STORIES

831 Stories

An imprint of Authors Equity
1123 Broadway, Suite 1008
New York, New York 10010

Cover design by C47
Book design by Scribe Inc.

This is a work of fiction. Names, characters, places, and incidents either are products of the author's imagination or are used fictitiously.

Library of Congress Control Number: 2026935587
Print ISBN 9798893311464
Ebook ISBN 9798893311471

Printed in the United States of America
First printing

www.831stories.com
www.authorsequity.com

For my younger self

I

PAIGE

To be fair, I did rent this cottage sight unseen. But when I step through a spider web to put the key in the door, it hits me that "charming vintage" was really just a pseudonym for "old and tired." The porch doesn't just creak; it sags. Inside, I'm confronted by a smell. It's distinctly damp. There are notes of mildewy towel and something old and papery, like books that haven't been read in decades. Books that look great from the outside but fall apart when you open them. It's not *not* a metaphor for my life. I feel a lump in my throat and force myself to swallow it, like taking a pill with nothing to drink.

Bobby follows behind me without talking, yawning and rubbing his eyes. We left Brooklyn early this morning, a week after his last day of second grade. I've never actually set foot in Sungold, New York, until today. But when I was a kid, I passed it every summer on the bus to camp in the Adirondack Mountains. My sister and I were the only girls from Idaho to attend, but our mom grew up going there, and for her, it was a whole thing.

"Is this where we're staying for the whole summer? Or is this just, like, on the way to where we're going?" Bobby asks me, his voice exasperated. He clearly is not impressed with the place either. He's a lot shocked and a little pissed. I've taken him away from everything he knows—including our townhouse with central air and a housekeeper who makes sure cobwebs never have a chance to accumulate—to this more-rustic-than-I-realized cottage. I've taken him from a city that pulses with life at every single intersection to this quiet house. The loudest sound outside of our windows is the buzzing of insects. My son's comfort is the collateral damage that's come with my desire to turn my life upside down.

I wish I had explained all of this better to him before we left. Not just where we were going for the summer but also why. I feel a swell of shame and sadness grow inside of me like a balloon filling to its capacity. I know I've done what's best for Bobby. I do.

And yet.

Keep it together, Paige, I think to myself. I put on a bright, brave smile, even though he's not facing me. Even though I could burst into tears. Faking optimism makes me feel like I'm able to punch a tiny hole in the balloon, momentarily deflating my rising anxiety.

"This is where we're going to be for the whole summer." I nod enthusiastically, like we're agreeing about something, hoping some of my artificial cheeriness will change his mood somehow. "It's our big summer adventure!"

"It's hot in here," he says, emphatically waving his hand to fan his face.

"We'll open some windows and get fans." I add "fans"

to my mental shopping list and lead him upstairs. "I think this place is actually so cute, don't you?" I pretend to gaze reverently at the two bedrooms and don't give him a chance to respond. "It reminds me of the bunks at my summer camp. I had the best time there, and I think you and I are going to have the best time here." I know I sound like a cheesy brochure. But I am trying. I really am.

"Whatever. Which room is mine?"

I tell him he can have whichever he wants. He picks the one to the right of the bathroom and slams the door behind him. I hear the thud of his backpack hitting the ground. He starts a loud roller-skating video on his brand-new iPad, a birthday present from his father. Even though his old one was perfectly fine.

I lean against Bobby's door and slide down it. I hold my head in my hands. At what point do I have to tell Jared that we made it upstate? What are the obligations of a trial separation? It's all proving to be more overwhelming than I allowed myself to imagine it would be. And I still don't think Jared gets how serious I am about this. Despite endless talks about all the ways things have changed between us, he somehow still thinks that I'm just taking Bobby off his hands for a couple of months, giving him an opportunity to gallivant with his friends on multiple sailing trips.

But we're here, Bobby and I, so I can see if I can really do this on my own. I'm finally taking the first step of a long-shot plan that has only ever existed in my mind. I thought stepping over the threshold of the cottage door would feel like turning a page to a new chapter of my life. It sounds cinematic, I know it does. It's just that I thought it would immediately feel exciting and liberating. But so far, it just feels dispiriting. And dusty.

Sweaty from lugging our bags inside, I decide to take a shower. Maybe I can wash the city and the last few hours off me and we can start fresh.

After stripping off my clothes in a pile on the floor (mental shopping list: "laundry bin"), I am thrilled to discover that the cottage has excellent water pressure. A small victory, but I'll take it. The shower sprays down hard on my shoulders, and I let out a huge sigh, equal parts relief and dismay. I wrap a towel around myself and stare in the mirror. My cheeks look shallow. The past few months of planning this separation have destroyed my appetite. I comb my long hair and run some product through it. I inhale the earthy, citrusy scent of vetiver and stare at my reflection. I try to look past my features to actually see myself through them. *I've actually done it*, I think as I breathe in the steam. *I've left.*

Twenty minutes later, I knock on Bobby's door, determined to turn this day around for him. To show him that being here really can feel like an adventure. "Hey, bud. Let's go check out the farmers' market. I bet there'll be cider donuts. And we can pick up pizza later for dinner." I'm not above bribing him with his favorite foods today.

"Fine. But when is Dad coming?"

Dad. I wish the word didn't feel like nails on a chalkboard. Does his dad remember to charge his Nintendo

Switch? Does he know what to pack for two whole months away? Does he search out a local day camp and remember all the forms? Does he think of cider donuts and pizza and know which chicken nuggets to buy for the freezer and which shampoo doesn't make Bobby's eyes sting? Of course not. Not that it's Bobby's job to give me any credit for this, but hearing him ask for his father at this moment is a special brand of hurt.

I force a smile and grab both the car keys and the ones for the rental house. They feel strange and heavy in my hand. "This summer is just you and me."

We drive the few miles into town in relative silence. Bobby continues to sulk.

The main street is shut down for the market, which is maybe a dozen tents at most. There are lots of people walking around. With our car windows open, we can hear the banjos from a bluegrass band. There are posters all over advertising a movie night in the local park. It feels like almost everyone, including us, is white. We're definitely not in the city anymore.

"Is this the whole thing?"

"Yep, things are a little smaller here than we're used to, huh?" Weekly trips to the massive Grand Army Plaza market every Saturday in Brooklyn have made Bobby a seasoned pro.

He looks at me with dismay. "You didn't bring any bags! I can't believe you forgot!" His face turns red, like he's going to either scream or cry. I know it's not about the bags.

I squat down to his eye level to reassure not just him but myself too. "Hey, it's OK. We'll figure out how to carry whatever we get, I promise. Why don't we find some donuts?"

"OK." He stomps off toward the donut stand, and I grin to myself that he's already identified it. While we wait in line, my phone buzzes. It's my assistant, Sofia, checking in for the second time this morning, even though it's a Saturday and even though she knows that I'm officially on sabbatical from running the publicity department at Wilmington Books. I don't have the energy to see what her text says. Anyway, there's no such thing as a true emergency in publicity, even if every hiccup can feel like one. I'll get back to her later and remind her who she should be getting in touch with instead.

"I can't decide between powdered sugar or cinnamon sugar."

"Sounds to me like you need one of each."

"Really? You always say I can only get one."

"Today we live a little." I wink at him. For the first time all day, he smiles. It's a tiny moment, but his reaction feels like clouds parting. Like maybe being here, even if it's hard for him and scary for me, will be OK.

Right before we get to the front of the line, my phone buzzes again. I swear I'm going to block Sofia if she doesn't let up. But it's my sister, Eve.

Just wanted to make sure you got there OK? Give B a kiss for me.

I smile. Eve, unlike most people in my life, knows this summer is a trial separation. She's maintained a healthy skepticism toward Jared since we started dating, long before we were ever married. His rich-guy sheen never really worked on her. She holds her tongue, but I know right now she's reminding me I'm not alone in this.

I text her back: *We're here.*

She responds: *What are you doing right now?*

Currently waiting in line for donuts at the farmers' market. Pretending to be chipper.

It's OK if you're not chipper. I'm proud of you P. You really did it.

I heart the text, let her words wash over me, then put my phone back in my pocket.

Mercifully, the donut vendor also has hot coffee. I get the largest cup they offer.

As we pay, I spot a line snaking around another tent. Everyone seems to be waiting to buy vegetables. The stand has a gigantic yellow sign with navy hand-lettering that says, "Two Peas Farm, born-and-grown in Sungold, New York." There's a Pride flag clipped to the stand's tent and another banner that says "Erase Racism."

"That place must be good, because they have the biggest crowd," Bobby says, and I feel a surge of pride. He's developing the kind of street smarts that belong to kids raised in cities. I wonder how being here in a small town will change that.

"Let's check it out," I tell him.

The entire booth is set up like a cookbook still life. There are worn gingham tablecloths with old wooden boxes sitting on their sides so the contents spill just so across the tables. Some hold red spring onions with the brightest purple skins, almost like beets. Others are filled with actual beets, their greens just as vibrant as the roots themselves.

There are multiple bins of zucchini, some green, others yellow, and more striped. There are greens upon greens, bunches of kale and rainbow chard with stems so bright and varied that they look like ribbon candy, a bucket of dill with feathery fronds blowing in the wind.

While Bobby eats his donuts, I listen to the conversations around me. It turns out one can learn a lot about Sungold by standing in this line. There's a heated town supervisor race, a guy threatening to buy the property where the swimming hole is, and a varsity basketball player who may or may not be getting recruited for UConn's women's team ("The next Natalie Czapski," someone says). Unlike at the markets in the city, no one seems to mind waiting here. It's as if this is where they want to be—in *this* line for *these* vegetables. It's not a stop on the way to where they need to be: It's the place.

As we get closer to the front, I realize why it's taking so long. The woman behind the register, who I know is Frankie because everyone keeps saying her name, is in no rush to move the line along. Every customer seems to want a moment with her. She knows everyone's names, including kids and dogs.

She has a big smile. She herself is big, probably twice my size. She seems unafraid to take up space. She has presence. Breadth. Her voice booms. She looks a little like Bridget Everett if Bridget Everett were more masc and sported short, dark hair with flecks of silver. She's got warmth. She looks like the friendliest person in the world.

As I get closer to the front, a twinkly older man greets her. "Morning, Frankie! I've got a new one for you!"

"OK, try me, Pete."

"How did the farmer repair her jeans?"

"I don't know, how?"

"With a cabbage patch!"

She chuckles. "That's a good one, Pete. I don't know how you come up with these. Let me ring up those for you." She takes his armload of produce. "You're finally going to try dandelion greens today?"

"I haven't been able to stop thinking about them since I overheard you tell someone to start the pot with bacon and end the whole thing with a splash of vinegar."

"I'm happy you're trying something new." She seems to really mean it.

The next customer also has a cooking question. "I'm having my neighbors over tomorrow night. How many bags of spinach do I actually need?"

Frankie seems invested in this question. She knows the neighbors that the customer is talking about. "Just them or the kids too? And is the spinach part of a dish, or are you just doing it on the side? Or a salad?"

I'm impressed with her patience. She could easily just sell as many bags of spinach as she wants, but she's really paying attention.

By the time it's our turn, I realize I've been so distracted by watching Frankie that I've forgotten to actually grab what we need.

"Um, sorry. I haven't picked anything out yet. Bobby and I just got here this morning. Sorry, this is Bobby, my son." I do a weird sort of Vanna White wave around him. "We're going to be here for the summer."

"Here at this booth?"

I laugh. She removes her sunglasses. They rest on her chest on a strap. The skin around her eyes is so much lighter than the rest of her face. It's clear she spends a lot of time outside.

"So what can I get you?"

"Ummmm. . . ." I pause, feeling suddenly anxious. "What do you recommend?"

Why am I acting like I've never seen a vegetable before? Why am I being so indecisive? Maybe decision fatigue has come for me at last. All the details about today, actually getting in the car and leaving Brooklyn and arriving here, have been looming in my mind for so long. All the things to remember to bring. All of the preparations at work to be able to step away. All of the conversations with Jared. All of the follow-up conversations I still need to have with Bobby. It's all been *so much*.

But something about being here under the Two Peas Farm tent feels calming. It feels safe. Happy. Taking it all in has allowed me to turn my brain off for a moment, so much so that I forgot why I've been standing in line.

"What do I recommend? That's like asking me to choose a favorite child."

Bobby looks up from his donuts. "I'm her favorite child." It's a joke between us, since he is, in fact, my only child.

Frankie laughs at that. "Would you like the Two Peas Special?" She points to a sign: *No Decisions Needed: 1 bunch kale, 1 pound carrots, 1 bag spinach, 1 pound zucchini, 1 bunch scallions + 1 bunch parsley.*

"Perfect."

Frankie just smiles at me. She gathers all of the produce on the table in front of her. Bobby tells her we forgot to bring a bag. I issue a string of apologies.

"It's no problem." Frankie pulls a paper sack from a stack behind her and piles the heavy stuff at the bottom and the more delicate items on top. "That will be twenty even."

"That's it?" These clearly aren't Brooklyn prices.

"Would you like me to charge you more?" She grins ear to ear.

"I'm just surprised. We're from the city."

"Which city?" she asks. I know she's ribbing me. Anyone here "from the city" is from the city I'm from, but sometimes I forget the entire world doesn't revolve around New York.

"Brooklyn," I say, like I'm admitting something.

"I've actually never been there."

"You've never been to Brooklyn?" Bobby is alarmed.

"Nope. Can you even believe it?" Her tone is sweet, not a hint of sarcasm.

"But we have the best pizza in the world!"

"I don't doubt that. But we have the best vegetables in the world."

"Pizza is so much better than vegetables."

Frankie just laughs, a truly generous response from a vegetable farmer. "Honestly, Bobby, you might be right about that."

As I pay, I realize the line has gotten even longer. Talking to Frankie made me feel like I was the only customer. "It was so nice to meet you. My name is Paige, by the way."

"It was nice to meet you, Paige."

Bobby and I both start to walk away, buoyed.

“Hey!” Frankie shouts after us. I turn. She’s holding up my bag. I forgot to take it.

I hurry back, blushing, and wave goodbye.

“Mom,” Bobby asks me, “can we go home now?”

II

FRANKIE

I stand with my feet as wide apart as I can get them and bend from the waist. With my right hand, I plunge my hori hori, which I think of as my farming dagger, into the soil and pull it back toward me to create a small hole. A farmer on my crew drops kale seedlings along the row as I go. I put one of the baby plants into the hole with one hand and use the other to cover it with the small mound of dirt I just dug up. It only takes me a few seconds to plant each one. The holes are close enough together that I can plant a bunch before I stand up and shuffle a few feet down to start the process all over again. Even though I'm only a fraction of the way through, my body is already feeling it. Only 190 more feet to go.

Mands, my second in command, walks over with their clipboard in tow.

I stand with one hand on my sacrum, massaging the spot that feels like an ever-tightening coil.

"How's your back?" they ask me.

"Oh, you know, terrible, but I wouldn't have it any other way."

"Have you thought about the waterwheel transplanter I emailed you?"

"It's cute that you think I check my email." I don't have a cell phone and my laptop has been on its last leg for years. My inbox is definitely not at the top of my list.

"Boss, I mean it. It could mean two people can plant at once—while seated. No one needs to bend. Plus, each plant gets a little bit of water right at its root when it goes in the ground so we wouldn't have to set up irrigation immediately."

I know all of this. I know what a waterwheel transplanter is and what its benefits are. And Mands knows I am stubborn. That's what being my right hand for almost a decade has taught them.

"I actually spoke to the supplier, and he said he'd give us a deal if we buy it along with those tractor implements I've been suggesting we get to help with cultivating. We don't have to be out there weeding everything by hand. We could save ourselves so much time—and people power—if we let a machine do it."

"Sure, but if we just let a machine plant our plants and weed them, too, what's next? Just automated everything? The whole point of Two Peas is that we do things the way we do them. And people love us for it."

"Frankie, people don't love Two Peas because we break our backs unnecessarily. They love us because we grow great vegetables and because of *you*. And they don't want to see you get totally burnt out."

We have had this conversation about a thousand times. But hearing it today as my back screams at me when I've only just started planting? Well, Mands's points are landing harder than usual. "I'll marinate on it. Anything else on your mind? Otherwise I'm going to finish this row."

"Yeah, actually, I have some bad news. You were right about Bex and River. They both just told me they're quitting."

I take a deep breath. I'm actually relieved I didn't have to fire them. "Honestly, that's not bad news. Neither of them seems to be able to cut it, and if they don't want to be here, I'd rather them not be." I don't mean to be harsh, but we have so much to get done that having folks on the crew who aren't eager to work really impacts the labor as well as everyone else's energy and moods. Farming really is just a series of putting things in the ground, pulling them out, and then putting them back again—you have to love the repetition. It's increasingly hard to find people who are up for it.

"There is some good news."

"Yeah?"

"They're in love with each other. And they're grateful to Two Peas for bringing them together. And now they're leaving to drive across the country."

"Adorable."

Later that day, I do the thing I always do when I'm in a pickle. I call my best friend Abby.

"Hold on!" she yells as she picks up. I can tell she's put me on speaker phone. "I am elbow deep in tuna salad!"

"Lovely."

I hear some commotion in the background, like a stack of metal bowls has collapsed in a sink or something. "What's up?" I can tell by the sounds and her tone that now's not a great time and she's probably in the middle of getting lunch ready. Abby runs the cafeteria at Sungold Elementary School all year, including over the summer for the kids who go to the camp there.

"I was just calling to say hi."

"You've never done that once in your life."

Abby knows me better than I even know myself and has since we met in kindergarten at the very school where she now works. "Fine, there is something," I admit.

"Go on." I can just about hear her smirk.

"Two kids on my crew fell in love with each other and decided to ditch the rest of the season so they could drive to California or something."

"That sucks. Not the falling in love part, just the abandoning you at the height of the season part."

"Anyway, I'm wondering if you know anyone looking for work? At least for the next month or so."

"I can't think of anyone off the top of my head," Abby says, "but this would really be a place to use social media."

"But what about good old word of mouth?"

"Of course, but it could let you cast a wider net. I'm just saying—"

I cut her off. I realize I'm pacing around my living room. "I know, I know."

"Well, in the meantime, I could share a job description with all the parents if you want. Just send me something and I'll include it with my weekly menu email."

“That would be amazing, Abs. I’ll get that to you by the end of the day.”

“Typed?” She knows how analog I am and how likely I am to drop off a piece of paper.

“I’ll even type it up for you.”

“By the way, what does Mands think?” I hear her mixing something in the background.

“They think if we get new equipment, we don’t need more people. But I’d rather pay people than pay for a hunk of metal.”

“Mands is just looking out for you.”

“Yeah, well, I’m old-school,” I say with a little disdain in my voice.

She laughs. “Oh, we know.”

III

PAIGE

I've just pulled up outside of Sungold Elementary, a one-story brick building with a playground in front and a small garden off to the side. We're early for Bobby's first day at camp. There are just a few kids running around outside.

My phone buzzes. I turn the screen around to face me and see that it's a text from Jared. It's a shirtless selfie of him on a boat somewhere. No *Hello*. No *How are you?* No questions about our son.

I belligerently type a response: *I'm dropping Bobby off for his first day of camp.*

Give him a Big Papa fist bump!

I will not, in fact, participate in anything called a "Big Papa fist bump." But I turn to Bobby, who has been watching me roll my eyes as I text.

"Who is it? Is it Dad?"

"He's just checking in."

"Tell him I miss him! Actually, can we call him?"

"We can call him later after camp." I'm actively trying to hide my annoyance. I know this is all hard enough for Bobby.

Drop-off goes smoother than I thought it would. Bobby has been itching to be around other kids.

Then I'm alone for the first time since we got to Sungold. And I am exhausted. It's only been five days, but I'm not used to spending this much one-on-one time with Bobby. Usually our schedule is filled with piano lessons and birthday parties and playdates. If I can't take him because of work, his nanny does. And while we're all out and about, our housekeeper is either tidying the house or washing clothes or prepping our meals.

Here in Sungold, I'm doing laundry and making dinner and trying to keep Bobby entertained all at the same time. It's what I wanted, yes, but it's also tiring. I've been craving a quieter life, a simpler life, a life away from the hamster wheel I've put myself on, away from Jared's control and his money that enables it. Now that I'm starting to get a taste of the simple life, I'm realizing that while it may be less chaotic, it's not less busy. I'm just occupied with more domestic, mundane things.

When Bobby was born, I felt whole in a way I never knew, felt aware of how many pieces of myself were floating before then and were finally able to click into place. Being a mom, being *his* mom, focuses me and my decisions like nothing else. While a lot of my life has felt shaky, being a parent never has. I always knew that I wanted to be one from the moment I had my first Cabbage Patch Kid. Taking care of someone, being responsible for them, brings out the best in me. It's where I can use my problem-solving skills, the role where I most feel the strength of my spine.

But the reality of being a mom is different from the fantasy I held my whole life. I honestly don't know how anyone could become a parent if they didn't know they were absolutely sure they wanted to be one. Sometimes it's so tedious, so full of boring and relentless questions. Questions from me: *Did you brush your teeth? But did you actually? Can you please tie your shoes?* And even more questions from him: *Do I have to? Where are my socks? Why do I have to? But why? Why? Why?* Parenting is repetitive. And tiring. Especially if your kid's other parent isn't as engaged as you are.

Before I turn my car on, I just hold the wheel and breathe out the particular type of sigh that all overtaxed parents know. I feel my shoulders drop an inch.

Then my phone rings. I brace myself for Jared. But it's my sister. My shoulders fall again.

"Eve! I'm so happy you called."

"Tell me how you're doing." It comes out as a demand.

I let out a small laugh.

"How's Bobby doing being away from his dad?" she asks.

"Honestly, it's so hard to hear how much he misses him. And it's hard to see him be so angsty about being here. And it's not like I want Bobby to hate Jared . . ." I am talking a mile a minute. Part of the problem is that the way Bobby talks about Jared is how *I* talked about Jared when I first met him. He can be so charming and can make you feel so safe. But those are just tactics. I know that now. And I now understand that having a trust fund and having your shit together are not the same thing. It took me longer than I wish it did to really get that. It's not that I didn't really love him at first; I just didn't see him clearly.

"Of course not. Go on," she says.

I take a deep breath. "Bobby's too young to understand that Jared has no idea what it means to actually show up in the day-to-day. He's like Santa Claus. He tiptoes in with presents and then leaves without taking responsibility for anything. He doesn't *parent* Bobby."

"Calling Jared 'Santa Claus' is way too generous," Eve says. "Sure they're both entitled straight white men who think they're in charge, but it implies that Jared's ever been jolly." I've never heard Eve say how she truly feels about Jared. I've sensed it, but it's never been confirmed with words. She's always just narrowed her eyes or responded with a low "hmmm" when I've complained. It's a little shocking and also validating to finally hear her say it all aloud.

Though there have been many signs, the turning point for me to take a true, physical step away from Jared was when he suggested we send Bobby to boarding school, something he always wished his parents had done for him. It's not that boarding school is inherently bad, but it's not the upbringing I've ever wanted for Bobby, nor is it the type of atmosphere he'd actually thrive in. Bobby is a quirky, nerdy kid who is obsessed with roller-skating. He's sensitive, a big feeler who cries easily. He's not tough. And I love all of those things about him. I just don't think other boys at a fancy boarding school would.

Jared and I fought about it so much, and it became obvious that Jared's idea of parenting is to give Bobby what he wished he had rather than actually make decisions based on what's best for Bobby. His concept of raising our soft boy is to harden him, to ship him off and watch him come home crisp collared and interested in lacrosse.

And it's not just the way we differ in parenting. It's also how we fight about it. How dismissive he is, how unwilling to think from a different perspective. I used to really admire Jared's steadfastness. The way his determination and confidence mixed was intoxicating to be around. It felt like everything was possible. Over time, I've learned that what I read as determination was mostly obstinacy. What seemed like confidence was mostly bluster.

I know it's been less than a week, but being away from Brooklyn, from our life, has already given me so much more clarity. But to say these thoughts out loud to Eve makes them all so much more real.

"Listen," Eve continues, "I never trusted him. Not from day one. I tried for so long to be supportive. Especially because you seemed taken care of, at least materially. That fucking townhouse! But now that you've actually gotten out, it's really hard for me to hold it in anymore."

It takes me a moment to let this all sink in. How long this has been going on.

"Paige, are you still there? I'm sorry, but I just couldn't *not* say all of that."

"I'm here." I clear my throat. "I'm sorry you've felt like you had to hold back for so long."

"I'm sorry you've felt so alone. And probably trapped."

I feel her words in my gut, in my throat. Tears start to run down my face.

"Anyway, I really just wanted to check in. I am so proud of you, and I'm here for you. You're not by yourself in this. And also: You're Bobby's mom, not his friend. It's OK if you're not his favorite person right now. You're doing the right thing. The most loving thing."

When we hang up, I take a minute to blot my tears before I pull out of the parking lot. Soon I'm on the long country road that leads to our unremarkable cottage. I roll down my windows and turn the volume up on the stereo. I make my steering wheel into a snare drum. I nod my head vigorously to the electric guitar. The song's energy is building. I crank the volume as high as it goes just in time for when the lyrics kick in. "*Wake up!*" I yell the first line of the song into the void. The car vibrates with sound.

The fact that I know every word to every System of a Down song isn't anyone's first guess about me. I give off soft pop vibes more than heavy metal. More messy top bun and pink cardigan than sweaty hair and faded black tee. But when I was in high school and first learned to drive, I discovered the private thrill of shouting along to *Toxicity* by myself in the car. The music made me feel like I could crack myself open. Like I could yell myself into a slightly dissociated state and just escape everything. Let it all out. I'd throw my armload of AP math textbooks into the passenger seat, release the elastic from my tight ponytail, and drive far enough away from the parking lot so that no one I knew could see me. Then, and only then, I'd scream-sing the lyrics, my voice turning to gravel and thunder.

Now more than twenty years later, the steering wheel starts to wobble and my heart drops. I know the sensation of a flat tire and manage to pull the car to the side of the road, the back left side thumping along. "Just my luck," I mumble to no one.

When I turn off the engine, the quiet feels abrupt. I get out and confirm what I already know, then pull out my phone to call for help only to find that I do not have service. Also my phone is about to die.

The road is empty in either direction, and the nearest building is falling down. I climb back into the driver's seat, tell myself that I will not cry and I will figure this out, that I am strong and independent and can do this. That I am a mother and a boss and I am the adult in charge here. Then I put my head in my hands and sob. I know it's not just about the tire.

How long can I sit here? What's the ticking clock for being stranded and alone? If I can get a bar of service, can I call AAA? Do I even have AAA?

My ears perk up at something noisy coming toward me on the road. As it gets closer, I realize it's the sound of loose tools banging around the bed of a pickup truck. I see the vehicle slowing in my side-view mirror. Before I can pull myself together, dab my eyes, and get out of my car, the door of the pickup opens. It's Frankie. She's in cargo shorts and boots, a gray tank top that probably started off as white, and a worn-in flannel shirt. She has a bandana tied around her neck that I'm sure has some practical purpose, but all I think is: *jaunty.*

She taps my window a couple of times. "You OK in there?" Her voice is loud, like I haven't noticed her. Like it's possible not to notice a six-foot-tall woman standing on the other side of a pane of glass.

I try to smile, try to make my face appear like I'm not someone stranded on the side of the road having a total emotional breakdown. But I know my eyes are giving me away. I stop pretending and let it happen: I start crying again.

"May I?" Frankie says as she opens my car door, not waiting for my response. "Are you hurt?"

I shake my head no.

"Just stuck here?"

I nod yes.

"Can I at least help you with that tire?" Her tone is so warm.

"Oh, you don't have to," I say. I use my sleeve to wipe my nose. "I can figure it out. Would you mind just lending me your phone? I don't have any service, and my battery is nearly dead." I'm trying to exude calm and confidence, but I know I'm not succeeding.

"I would lend it to you, but I don't have a cell phone." Frankie shrugs, as if that's the most normal thing in the world.

"I'm sorry—you don't have a phone?"

"I have a phone. It's plugged into the wall at my house."

"A landline?" I am trying to remember the last time I used an actual landline.

"Yes, a landline." She laughs a little, as if my disbelief is the weird part of this exchange.

"But what if there's an emergency? What if you get a flat tire and no one drives by to help you?"

"I have a spare tire." She winks at me. "C'mon, let's get yours, and we'll get you fixed up so you can get on your way."

"Like actually change the tire ourselves?" Again I am in disbelief.

"Yes, like *actually*." She gently mocks me. "It'll be fun."

"If you're sure it's not an inconvenience . . ." I trail off, as though I have other options.

"Well, I'm here, and I'm not in a rush. And you know what's better than two hands?"

I just look at her quizzically.

"Four hands!" It's a ridiculous thing to say, and I laugh. Her enthusiasm would be annoying if it wasn't so genuine.

We walk to the trunk of my car and lift up the floor covering. And that's when we both see the gaping hole where the spare should be.

"Jesus!" I let out an exasperated huff. I shake my head in annoyance as I remember that Jared removed the spare a few months ago to put in our home gym so he could use it in his workouts—something about elevating his feet, or his hands, when he does push-ups.

I close my eyes, hoping that when I open them, the scene will magically reset. But of course this is how it is. Somehow Jared can fuck up my day without even being here. I turn to Frankie. "My . . . my, um . . ." I grit my teeth. Start again. "Bobby's dad took the tire out for . . ." I can't figure out how to explain the absurdity.

"Your husband?"

"Yes. But it's complicated. I'm here in Sungold for the summer testing out what life would be like not being married to him." The tears redouble behind my eyes, but I let the words flow from me instead. "He knows things aren't great between us, obviously, but he doesn't quite know how much I want this separation to stick. And Bobby just thinks we're having a fun summer away. Not that he's really been having that much fun. I just dropped him off at camp and am hoping that helps." I let out a breath. I feel like I have been talking for a month. Why am I treating this like a confessional?

"That does sound complicated." Frankie nods. "Hold on a second." She goes back to her pickup and unearths something from the crowded truck bed. She pulls out a tire and a few tools.

"Do you know how to use a lug wrench?"

"Frankie, I'm flattered you think I even know what those two words mean on their own, let alone together," I tell her with a laugh.

She holds out a metal X-shaped tool in my direction. She pokes me in the arm with it. "It doesn't bite."

I smile and take it from her.

"OK, first, pry off the hubcap, and then you'll use the wrench to loosen the lug nuts. I'll walk you through the whole thing."

"Look, I don't want to ask you to do this by yourself,

but wouldn't that be easier than teaching me? I don't want to take up your whole day."

"What's the fun in that? And what happens if you get another flat tire one day and I don't happen to just pull up in my truck next to you?" she asks.

I take a deep, fortifying breath. "OK, so how do I pry off a hubcap?"

"Here, pass me the wrench and I'll get it started and you can finish the job." She places the flat end of the wrench in the small groove between the hubcap and the inner edge of the tire and begins to gingerly pry it away. "Your turn."

I take the wrench in my hands and finish pulling the hubcap away. It comes off easily. More easily than I imagined it would.

"I did it!" I say it like it's a bigger win than it is.

"You did it!" There's not an ounce of derision in her tone, but I can't be totally sure.

"Are you making fun of me?"

"No, why would you think that?"

"I just couldn't tell if you were being sarcastic. Taking off a hubcap is probably not a big deal for you."

"I'm definitely not making fun of you, but I am getting a kick out of you. Being a farmer means that ninety-nine percent of my job is fixing broken things. I don't really celebrate when I fix them. You're reminding me that it feels good to do that."

"Well, I'm glad I could at least offer you something from this disaster."

"Oh, this isn't a disaster. But then again, I'm used to

things falling apart." She pauses. "I'm getting the sense that most things in your life don't fall apart all of the time?"

I let out a laugh. "Well, that's where you're wrong. My whole life is basically a flat tire right now. What gave you the impression that I have it all together? My endless stream of tears, my dead cell phone, or my complete ineptitude with tools?"

She laughs. "I don't know—you just look very put together."

I peer down at my clothes. My pressed T-shirt. My crisp jeans. She has a point.

"Looks can be deceiving."

She nods seriously, as if I'm the first person to ever say these words. And I realize, at this moment, that as soon as I wash these clothes, they will stay wrinkled. There's no way I'm going to take up ironing.

Then the wrench slips out of my hand and lands right on my foot.

I yelp more loudly than I need to. It doesn't hurt that badly; it just surprises me.

Frankie looks at me with concern. "Do you want to, like, I don't know, sit down and just hang out while I fix this? I thought showing you would be fun, but maybe you just need a break?"

My fingertips come to my chest without me realizing it. "Honestly, that would be amazing."

She nods toward a fallen log on the side of the road. I perch on it. I take a deep breath and close my eyes for a moment. When I open them, Frankie is working on the tire, and I can't seem to look away.

I am mesmerized by her competence, the way each tool seems like an extension of her hand. Her body looks so sturdy. Even though she's large, she moves fluidly, not wasting a step between her truck and my tire. She crouches up and down from the ground with buoyancy. I marvel at how effortless all this effort seems to be for her. She rolls up the sleeves of her flannel, and her forearms are striking not just because they're covered in tattoos but also because they are so strong. When she squeezes her wrench, I can see her muscles flex involuntarily.

I find it hard to look away. Watching her work settles me. It's as if all the emotions that have been boiling over inside of me come to a gentle simmer. I feel . . . warm?

Frankie places a jack under the car and then, like magic, lifts the whole thing up off the ground. I know it's not actually her strength that lifted the car, but it may as well have been. She removes the flat and finds where a rusty nail has punctured the rubber.

"This should be fairly easy to patch at the shop." Frankie wipes a little sweat off her brow with her sleeve. Her cheeks and neck have gone a little pink, and my eyes track to the collar of her shirt. "I'll just pop the spare on for now, then you should head over to the mechanic on Elmwood. Tell him Frankie sent you and that I said not to rip you off."

"I don't know how to thank you—" I start as Frankie finishes up and throws her supplies back into the bed of her truck.

"It's no big deal," she interrupts and unties the bandana from around her neck to wipe her hands clean. "I should get on the road."

Then she puts her hand on my shoulder and gives it an assured squeeze, as if to say *everything's going to be all right.*

There's something about Frankie touching me. I feel the squeeze from my shoulder all the way to my toes.

A few hours later, I am pulling out of the cottage driveway with a patched tire, Bobby's roller-skating bag, and mine too.

"How about we skate before we go home for dinner?" I ask him when he gets in the car at camp pickup.

"Both of us?" His eyes are big and eager.

"Yeah, both of us. I haven't used mine in too long." I point to the gear in the back seat.

"Yes!" He buckles his seat belt hurriedly as if that will get us there faster.

We go to the empty parking lot behind the neighboring high school. Bobby laces up his skates, puts on his knee pads and helmet, and speeds by me. He starts practicing his crossovers and bunny hops.

I just skate leisurely and enjoy the evening sun. I turn on some music on my phone and put it in my back pocket. I make big, loopy circles. I feel my toes unclench, my arms loosen along my sides.

Eventually we get back in the car, both of us a little tired and noticeably calmer than we were when we got here. I need to remember to do this more often.

On the way home, I call in an order for Chinese food and drive toward the restaurant.

"We're picking up dinner? Why can't we just use an app to get it delivered?" He's incredulous.

"Bobby, you're not going to believe this, but the world operated for a long time without apps."

He rolls his eyes at me, and I get a glimpse of him as a teen. But it's better than him crying or yelling at me. I try to hide my smile.

The next morning after camp drop-off, I go to Two Peas Farm to return the spare tire Frankie lent me. I walk past a ramshackle shed toward a bunch of farmers standing in a small huddle in a field. Frankie is talking to them, her back to me, explaining some task they're about to do. As I get closer, I hear, "Work in pairs, because you know what's better than two hands?"

"Four!" they all shout back. She's clearly in her natural habitat.

I approach the group. "Hi, sorry, I don't mean to interrupt—"

Frankie turns around. "Hey, Paige!"

"That mechanic was great. He told me where the farm is. I hope it's OK I'm here? I brought your tire back. It's in my trunk."

"Oh, good. You can just throw it in the back of my truck." She nods toward her pickup in a patch of mud. I turn with a wave, trying not to think about my pristine sneakers. *You can wash them*, I remind myself.

I start to walk away, feeling aware that I'm sad our

interaction was so brief. I don't exactly know what I want from her, but I felt so comfortable with her yesterday, even in such a vulnerable state. I guess I just want more of that comfort. And company. Plus, I'm feeling more myself today, and I want her to know I'm not a total mess.

"Actually, Paige!" Frankie shouts.

I look back. "Yeah?"

"Want to join us for lunch? We were going to take our break soon."

I attempt to play it cool even though, on the inside, I'm buzzing. "Sure, that'd be great."

Frankie calls over a tall, androgynous farmer. "Mands, you can handle the rest of this until lunch, right?"

"Sure thing. While they finish this section, I'm going to take the new wheel hoe into those beds in the north field."

"I thought we said we'd do that tomorrow so we can get at least three people on the job?"

"Nope, the new wheel hoe is battery operated. I'll get it done in less than half the time the old hand-pushed ones take. And by myself."

Frankie rolls her eyes. "OK, fine. How about this? If you get all of the beds done by the end of the day, I'll consider that water contraption thing."

Mands reaches out their hand. "Shake on it?"

Frankie reluctantly clasps palms, then turns back to me.

"OK, Paige, you're going to be my sous-chef." Frankie strides toward the small Cape Cod–style house at the far end of the farm, past the cars. She's walking fast, and I'm trying hard to keep up.

"What was that all about?"

"Oh, nothing. Mands is always pushing me to modernize things around here. You just witnessed our recurring bit."

I follow her into her house.

It's like a time capsule. The low ceilings and framed paintings of fish and mountains on the walls remind me of my grandfather's house back in Idaho. There's the softest-looking couch I've ever seen with an old quilt thrown over it and an even older-looking dog sleeping on top.

"That's Fran."

"Your dog's name is Fran?" I bite my lip. I plead with myself not to laugh.

"Yes."

"And you're Frankie?"

"Yes."

I laugh anyway.

"She came with her name from the rescue place, and I didn't have the heart to change it. Anyway, she's old and she mostly sleeps all day. She used to run around the farm and come with me everywhere, but these days she just prefers to hang out here."

"I get it. If I could lie on that couch all day, I would probably do the same."

Frankie smiles. "Why don't you sit with her while I get everything out for lunch. I'll call you when I'm ready for help." She takes off her flannel shirt, ties it around her waist, and turns toward the kitchen. I notice how broad and muscular her shoulders are. Maybe she did lift that car after all?

I nod and plop down next to Fran. At first she barely

moves, but after a moment, she turns ever so slightly to offer her belly to me, as if it's a gift that I get to rub. I happily oblige.

"Paige!" Frankie calls. "You're up."

I follow the sound of her voice to the kitchen, which is small but absolutely perfect. One wall is a giant pegboard filled with pots and pans and tools. Like Julia Child's. There's a picture window over the sink, and I can see the whole farm through it. Frankie is standing next to the sink rinsing off a pile of gigantic bright-red tomatoes. She points to a cutting board and serrated knife waiting for me on her hulking wooden kitchen island.

"OK, you're on tomato slicing," she tells me. "Thick. We're having tomato sandwiches."

"Oh, like the Spanish tomato toast thing? What's that called again? Pan con tomate?"

"I'm sure that's great, but no. We're doing old-fashioned tomato sandwiches with soft white bread and lots of mayo and enough salt and pepper to make you sneeze. Best food in the world."

"But there's that great bakery next to you at the market?" I'm wondering aloud why someone so devoted to great vegetables would use grocery-store white bread.

"Paige. Just trust me."

I smile and get to slicing.

The tomatoes are so deep red inside that I can't resist tasting a piece, and my eyes bulge when I do. "How are these so good and it's still just June? Usually I don't get ones like this until later in the summer at the market."

"Good observation," she says and nods approvingly. "A

few years ago we switched from growing them outside, where it doesn't get warm enough for them to really get going until later in the season, to inside one of our high tunnels. This way we can control the temperature and get better yields."

"Was that a Mands suggestion?"

"As a matter of fact, it was." She smiles. "Actually, it's still early for ripe tomatoes like these. These precocious ones are just for us farmers. We don't have enough to sell at market yet, but I could never waste these."

"Honestly, I feel honored. Thanks for sharing them with me."

"Do you want to see the tunnel? I can show you after lunch."

I blush at the invitation, which feels distinctly flirtatious, and also because I'm a bit embarrassed about how little I know. "I've actually never been to a vegetable farm. Only ever to the market."

"People like me need people like you," Frankie says with a wink.

OK, yes, she's definitely flirting, and I definitely didn't have flirting with a farmer, let alone a butch woman farmer, on my list of plans for the summer. I notice my breathing is shallow. This whole train of thought is unexpected but exciting too. I keep my eyes trained on my cutting board. When I let myself look over at Frankie, she's spreading more mayonnaise on slices of bread than I knew slices of bread could hold, and there's a mountain of sandwiches accumulating.

"How many people work for you?" I ask her.

"Oh, not as many as you would think from this tower. There're just six of us, seven with you. But a well-fed crew is a happy crew." She stacks the sandwiches and a large jar of pickles on a tray. "Mind carrying this so I can get Fran? And potato chips?"

"Of course." But the tray turns out to be much heavier than I anticipated, and Frankie notices me straining to carry it.

"Want to switch?"

"No, I got it!" I put a big smile on my face. *Don't drop this*, I tell myself. It feels important, somehow, to show her I can handle this one thing.

We walk over to a long picnic table alongside the shed, with a big shade cloth hanging overhead. We spread out our sustenance, and Frankie emerges from the shed with a roll of paper towels and a six-pack of cold seltzer cans.

As I crack one open, her crew descends. They are all talking over each other, carrying their conversations from the field to lunch. They rip paper towels off a roll to use as plates and grab sandwiches and fistfuls of chips. Some of them nod at me, but most of them are oblivious—and ravenous.

Frankie has everyone go around the table to introduce themselves to me. As lunch carries on, I can't help but notice that sitting here feels incredibly familiar. Almost like I've been here before, even though I definitely haven't.

And then it hits me. It's like I'm back at sleepaway camp and it's lunchtime and I'm with my whole bunk. It feels just as wholesome and communal.

Joking around with Frankie and her crew, all of us

passing the party-size bag of chips back and forth and laughing, it dawns on me that this kind of easygoing sociability has been sorely lacking in my life. Things with Jared got so tense in the last year or so. Dancing around his moods and avoiding conflict became so all-consuming that my world had gotten smaller and smaller. And it hasn't just been him. Outside the house, I was mostly at work, where everyone takes everything so seriously, or at Bobby's school, where all of the other moms are constantly gossiping behind each other's backs.

I've missed this kind of relaxed, jovial interaction where everyone is aligned about the stakes. And Frankie is at the literal head of the table, setting the tone and making this atmosphere possible. It's comfortable and comforting, plus it's undeniably hot to see her in control.

I take a sandwich off the tray and bite into it. As I chew, I close my eyes in appreciation. "How is something this simple so good?" I'm not really expecting an answer, just thinking out loud.

"Told you." Frankie grins, and now that I'm this close to her, I can see that her front tooth is a little bit chipped. I'm sure I've sat across from countless people with imperfect teeth without thinking twice about it, but with Frankie? I don't know why, but I can't stop staring at her tooth and at the mouth that holds it. I find myself fascinated: How long has it been like this? Did she bump it on something? Bite something too hard? Is it sharp when she runs her tongue over it? There is a whole world in that tooth. I want to know everything about it.

IV

FRANKIE

"You've never brought a conquest to the farm," Mands says.

We're walking out to the brassica field after lunch to check the cabbages, cauliflower, and broccolini for any signs of insect damage and to see how bad the weeds are. We're trying to stay extra vigilant this year.

"I would never call a woman a *conquest*. And even if I did, she's not."

"Seriously? You two definitely have chemistry."

"We do not," I say, perhaps a little too defensively. Mands is not wrong, though. I think Fran even sensed the tension between me and Paige.

"OK, but you have to admit she's your type." Mands is not going to let this go.

They're also not wrong. When I was fourteen, I ripped a picture of Cindy Crawford out of a magazine and taped it up inside my closet. I didn't quite understand the feelings she elicited in me then, but soon enough I figured it out. Ever since, I've always been drawn to conventionally attractive women. Symmetrical features and blow-dried hair just do it for me—what can I say?—and Paige fits the mold. She has a glow like people with skin care routines tend to. I bet her white T-shirts don't come in multipacks like mine do.

"Sure, Paige is beautiful. But she's also definitely straight and definitely married."

Mands smirks. "That's what I mean. Exactly your type."

"Very funny."

"Well, who is she? What's her deal?"

I tell Mands about meeting her at the market and fixing her tire. "And no, I'm not trying to sleep with her. I just figured it would cost me literally nothing to make an extra tomato sandwich."

What I don't share with Mands is the way Paige was looking at me while I fixed her tire, like I was a long menu at a diner and she was trying to figure out her order. Trying to figure out what she craved. I leave out that I liked how it felt to be so considered. So studied.

I know that particular look from seemingly straight women. It's the face they make when they're trying to determine what that funny feeling is inside of them, before they realize it's simply desire. Maybe it's a different type of desire than they're used to, sure, or maybe it's the kind they've always known they've had deep down, but they've been able to ignore it.

Here's how it typically goes for me: A woman will come to the market, obviously an out-of-towner, and we'll have a little banter at the register. She'll ask me if there's anywhere good to get a drink around here, I'll tell her about Sam's, and then I'll inevitably see her there later that evening when I go in for my postwork beer. After all, it's the only watering hole in town. She'll say something like

"Funny seeing you here," and I'll buy her a drink, then she'll buy our second round. We'll talk and flirt, and I'll see her silently negotiate whether she's going to let herself experience this thing she's always wondered about. And then I'll say I have to get home to Fran, which will break her heart, but then I'll explain that Fran is my dog, and she'll say, "I love dogs," and I'll say, "Want to meet mine?"

It's not always that exact exchange. But it's something close, nine times out of ten.

And this arrangement works just fine for me. It allows me to have really fun, no-strings-attached sex maybe once a month, give or take, which is just enough to keep me *animated* but not so much that it gets in the way of my life. It also means every time I have sex, it's accompanied by the excitement of someone new. The anticipation, the crescendo, the skillet of bacon and eggs in the morning. And then they leave, and I never have to deal with anything messy like feelings, or last names, or god forbid, actual relationships. Sleeping with people who don't stick around is how I stay committed to my three true long-term relationships: the farm, Fran, and my best friend.

"Well, she was really nice." Mands squats down amid the broccolini and snaps me back to the present moment. "She's welcome to come for lunch anytime."

It's Monday night, which means Abby and I are getting hamburgers like we've done nearly every week since she moved back home a few years ago when she decided working at restaurants in the city wasn't quite what she imagined it would be.

During the winter, we sit in the corner booth at Sam's, but come this time of year, we sit outside at Lakeside Cones. Most people come just for ice cream, but true locals know that Raj, who runs it, is the best short-order cook in Sungold. He makes the batter for his onion rings with local beer and can manage a dozen smashburgers at the same time. He even makes his own spice blend for his masala fries, a secret family recipe that I've tried to pry out of him for years to no avail.

Today Abby has arrived before me and is already in line. She tells me to find a table, that it's her week to pay.

When she joins me, she hands me a glass bottle of Coke and clinks hers with mine. "They said it shouldn't be too long."

"It's not like I'm in a hurry—where else would I need to be?"

"You probably have plans to go back to the farm after dinner to pull weeds with a headlamp on."

We laugh and roll our eyes at each other. I ask her how camp is going, who her pickiest eaters are this year. Abby elbows me. "Don't try to change the subject."

"I just don't really feel like talking about my failing business at the moment." I try to keep my tone light, but she can probably sense the weightiness underneath. Right now, my to-do list feels like a burden, like a list of tasks that won't necessarily lead to success.

There's always a lot to do on the farm, but early summer is especially hard. So much of what we planted in April is ready to harvest, and we're also getting everything in the ground for the fall, our busiest time of year. It's a lot to keep up with. Even if I manage to hire new people to cover for the two farmers who quit, then I have to train them. And pay them. And we never have as much money coming in as we seem to need. Every year feels like rolling the dice.

"Your business isn't failing, Frankie. It all depends on how you define success." I can tell one of her "life lessons" is coming my way. "Wait—" She takes a long pull of her soda. "How *do* you define success? I don't think I've ever actually asked you that."

"Making a profit? Getting to pay everyone fairly and having enough leftover at the end so I can keep Fran in the lavish lifestyle she's accustomed to?"

"Is that a question or an answer?" Abby asks.

"An answer. Yes, success is being able to make enough money to make it all work."

"That makes sense," she says, "but I do think there's more to it than that. It's not just money. If success is being beloved in the community—which I think is at least part of it—then you're probably the most successful business in Sungold."

"Thanks, Abs. And I don't take that for granted. But being beloved doesn't help me fix a broken tractor or give everyone a raise. I know people here would rally around Two Peas if there were some kind of emergency. But that's just it: I don't want there to have to be an emergency to get financial support, do you know what I mean?" I breathe out a long sigh. I wish our burgers were ready so I'd have an excuse not to talk about this.

"I do know what you mean. And I also know that I don't run a business, so I don't actually know what it feels like to be in your shoes."

"I do like being the boss, so there's that."

"That's true, you barely tolerated having a teacher in elementary school, so I can't imagine you working for anyone now."

"Abby!" Raj yells. I'm saved by the bell, and we're both ravenous enough that our conversation halts while we take the first bites of our cheeseburgers, fully loaded with all of the toppings. We dip our onion rings in the Lakeside Cones sauce, which has something special in it that no one can identify (I'm almost positive it's Worcestershire and perhaps a tiny pinch of fenugreek, but Raj won't tell me if I'm right).

"You didn't answer my question earlier," I say.

"Which question?"

"About the kids."

She laughs. "We have one who won't even eat the chicken nuggets because they aren't dino shaped. But most of them are easy."

"What was on the menu today?"

"Pulled chicken tacos, rice and beans, and some of your lettuce with that lime dressing I make sometimes." I know the one she's talking about. She blends fresh lime juice and zest with garlic, honey, and olive oil. It's deceptively simple and so good.

I love hearing Abby talk about her job. She seems so happy working at the school. Unlike me, Abby left Sungold as soon as she could. Literally the day after our high school graduation, she moved to the city to work in fancy restaurants. After a few years, though, the grueling schedule and low pay wore her down, and she decided to move back home. Or at least that's what she told me. This was also right when my dad got sick, and I was struggling to run the farm and be his caretaker at the same time. Abby moved in with us to help for the last month of his life. After he died, I thought Abby would go back to the city. But then the longtime lunch lady retired, and Abby thought maybe cooking at the school would be a great way to get back to food without the crazy schedule and intensity of a restaurant kitchen. And now she lives five minutes away and we get to have dinner every Monday.

After we polish off our burgers, we get back in the line to order ice cream, and someone taps my shoulder. It's Paige with her son.

"Hi!" I feel myself beaming at her. Bobby nods at me, then stares at Abby like he's trying to place her.

"I swear I'm not following you around Sungold," Paige says, blushing. "We just finished dinner at home, and I thought we could use a little ice cream nightcap."

"It's the best." Abby reaches out her hand to introduce herself.

"You're the lunch lady!" Bobby says.

"That's me!"

Paige lights up. "Well, I think you'll appreciate knowing that the first thing Bobby said when I picked him up today was 'I had salad and actually liked it!'"

"Is that so?" Abby smiles, inclining her head toward Bobby.

"Yeah, and I ate, like, four tacos."

"Music to my ears."

Paige insists on paying for our dessert. "It's the least I can do to thank you, Abby, for getting my son to eat something green and for helping me with that tire, Frankie." She reaches out and touches my elbow as she says this, and I feel a tingle through my entire arm. I will myself to settle.

As Paige orders, I quickly explain the tire saga to Abby, who just lifts one suspicious eyebrow in reply. "She's your type," Abby whispers to me while Bobby convinces Paige to let him have something blue with various bits of candy and cookies mixed into it.

"Keep your voice down," I whisper back. "There's no *there* there."

"Whatever you say." Abby gives me a funny little salute.

"Do you want to join us?" I ask Paige.

"Oh, that's so nice, but I don't want to interrupt your date."

Abby and I both start cackling. It's not the first time someone has thought we're a couple. "Best friends." Abby motions between us. "We're like sisters."

I can't tell if Paige really looks relieved or if I just want her to.

"Well," she begins and reaches out for my elbow again, "we should actually get going. I promised Bobby he could eat his cone in the car while we drive around and get to know the area a bit better. Got any recommendations for us?"

Abby suggests the loop around the entire lake.

"And if you go past Two Peas and make a left on Route 53, you'll get one of the nicest views in all of Sungold," I add.

"How far on Route 53?"

"Oh, you'll know it when you see it," I tell her with a wink. Abby gives me a look as if to check to see if I know I'm being flirtatious. I can't help it. It's just who I am.

"Do you have cows at your farm?" Bobby asks me.

"No, unfortunately not. Just vegetables. And a very sweet old dog named Fran."

"I love cows."

"I know a farmer with cows if you ever want to meet some up close."

"Really?"

"I never lie."

Paige smiles at me.

"Actually, Paige, take my number in case you ever want to arrange that. I'd be happy to set it up." I pull out the small notebook I always keep in my chest pocket and scribble my name and number on a piece of paper. When I tear it off and hand it to her, I notice Abby's eyebrows, which could not go farther north if they tried.

Paige takes my pen right out of my hand and writes her number down on my notepad. She hands it to me and grabs a stack of extra napkins for the road.

As soon as they're in the car, Abby turns to face me, her eyes wide. "Umm, she likes you."

"Yes, I am a very likable person. Don't sound so surprised."

"She *likes you* likes you. And you know it. She could not stop touching you."

"Oh, she does not like me like that," I reply, even though I don't totally believe what I am saying. I can still feel Paige's grip on my elbow. "And even if she did like me, I'm not looking for anything right now. I have to focus on the farm."

"You're never looking for anything, Frank. But I think someone is looking at you. And I can tell you like looking at her."

"Whatever. She's straight and married."

"Just your type."

"I need everyone to stop saying that."

V

PAIGE

I have gotten dressed for all sorts of things in my life: a black-tie wedding in Napa, business dinners at Michelin-starred restaurants in Manhattan, dates at small wine bars in Brooklyn. But I have never had to contemplate the appropriate outfit for harvesting garlic.

Frankie called me yesterday and asked if I wanted to come help her and her crew this afternoon for "one of the best days of the entire year." How could I turn that down?

I tug on what I usually wear for Pilates: leggings, a sports bra, and a tank top, all the same shade of sage green. I put on my oldest pair of sneakers, the ones I don't care as much about if they get dirty, and a solid black baseball cap.

I look at myself in the mirror. I definitely do not look like a farmer. I look like a rich Brooklyn mom who is on her way to get an overpriced latte made with nondairy milk and will order while talking into her AirPods. But I'm comfortable in what I'm wearing. I'm able to move and bend and do whatever it is you do when you harvest garlic. Besides, I'm not really a rich Brooklynite. I'm just married to one. One very wealthy man who has been extremely clear from day one that the money is his, not ours. It was all laid out in our prenup.

"Hey!" Frankie yells when she sees me round the corner to the garlic field. She's surrounded by her crew, and they're each wearing a version of the same thing she is: sturdy work pants and loose, lightweight long-sleeved shirts. I am the one thing that is unlike the others in this scenario.

I instantly feel nervous and, as I do when I feel nervous, like I need to fill the space with conversation. "Before I forget to tell you," I say to Frankie, "that spot on Route 53 you recommended was amazing. The mountains looked like a painting. Bobby even said, and I quote, '*Wowww.*'"

"Sometimes I drive Fran over to that lookout spot, and we just sit and watch the sunset."

"That's so romantic."

"I guess it is." Frankie smiles, and now that I've noticed her chipped tooth, it's all I can see.

Suddenly the image pops into my head: Me sitting next to Frankie in her truck, Fran between us, watching the sky change color. Where is this coming from? Could I be developing an actual crush? My slightly elevated heart rate feels like my body is nodding yes. I brush the feelings away, though. I'm at the farm to do something new, and I don't want to make a fool of myself because I'm lost in my head and not paying attention.

"Paige, you're going to be helping Suzzanne." Frankie introduces me to the farmer standing next to her, a very short, young Black woman who seems to be a very serious adult trapped in a college-aged body.

"Two *z*'s and two *n*'s," Suzzanne clarifies.

"I'll keep that in mind."

Suzzanne, emphasis on the consonants, passes me a tool that's half as tall as I am. She calls it a "forker," and it is basically a small pitchfork. She has one too. She shows me where to place it near the plants to loosen the soil around the garlic bulbs without actually touching them. "We're going to fork this row, you and me, and then the rest of the crew will follow us and pull the garlic."

I place the tines on the ground and push like Suzzanne showed me and absolutely nothing happens. She's facing me, on the opposite side of the row, so she sees my frustration.

"What's wrong?"

"Mine doesn't want to go in the ground like yours does."

"You just have to give it a lot of effort. If the ground is really hard, you can step on top of it to give it some extra oomph. Like this." Suzzanne demonstrates, and I mimic her.

Soon enough, I get the hang of it, but I'm nowhere near as fast as Suzzanne, who is flying down her side. Mands offers to switch spots with me.

"I'm sorry I'm so slow," I say, stepping aside.

"Don't be sorry! You're doing great, and you haven't nicked a single garlic bulb, which is more than Suzzanne can say, but that's between you and me."

I instantly feel less useless, and I can understand why Mands is Frankie's right hand. They have a warm sense of humor and an eagle eye. They have been monitoring not only the team's efficiency (or lack thereof, in my case) but also every single garlic bulb.

Mands lets out a big sigh and leans against the fork. "Honestly, loosening the bulbs this way is way more time-consuming than if we just undercut the whole bed."

"What does that mean?"

"It means attaching a big metal blade to the back of the tractor, dropping it into the ground so it's just under the garlic bulbs, and then pulling it all the way down the row. It loosens all the soil below the garlic in one swoop."

I think about how hard I had to dig to loosen a few bulbs. "That sounds great. Why don't you just do that?"

"Frankie likes to keep things old-school. And a part of me gets it. It's more precise and less wasteful to do it this way. If we undercut, we risk losing more bulbs. But what we would lose in garlic, we'd make up for in time and physical energy. But she's got a hard time letting go of doing things the way her dad did them." Mands clears their throat. "Anyway, I shouldn't be saying all of this to you."

I wave my hand to shoo off the thought. I want Mands to keep talking. I want to know more about how Frankie runs the farm and why she does things the way she does them. I want to know more about her dad. I want, I am realizing, to know whatever information anyone might want to give me about her.

Now that Mands is digging the garlic, I switch to what they were doing: collecting the harvested piles and carrying them to the back of Frankie's pickup truck. After a bit of trial and error, I learn to use my arms almost like the prongs on a forklift. As I walk each load of garlic to the truck, I pretend I'm in a workout class. I try to keep my posture straight and my shoulders back.

A half dozen trips later, with my arms piled so high that I can barely see where I'm going, my foot lands *just* so in a small hole, and the garlic and I go flying. I land hard on the ground, and I already know the back of my workout pants is covered in mud. I'm surrounded by garlic as if it were confetti.

I start laughing. Hysterically laughing. A few people come over to help pick up the garlic, and Frankie reaches out her hand and hoists me up. She wipes some dirt off my back.

"Sorry about that," I say without a tinge of embarrassment.

"Happens to the best of us." Frankie squeezes my shoulder, just like she did after she fixed my tire. The touch is brief but impactful. It feels reassuring and a little exciting too.

I get back to the job and feel a quiet sense of pride. I'm happy I said yes to this invitation, happy I showed up to do something I've never done with a group of people I barely know. I'm pleased that when I fell, I could laugh at myself and get right back up. It feels liberating and relaxing to loosen the tension on my buttoned-up life.

Suzzanne and Mands invite me to come with them to the greenhouse to set up the wooden racks where all of the garlic will cure. I guess everyone here already knew that garlic had to sit for at least a few weeks to dry out, but I sure didn't.

As we prep, I listen to Mands and Suzzanne talk about plants and gender.

"All of the solanaceous plants have perfect flowers, so—" Mand starts.

"Sorry, what does *solanaceous* mean?" I can't help but interrupt.

"Oh, it's just a fancy word for nightshades, for all the plants related to potatoes. Anyway, yeah, they have perfect flowers."

"Yeah, I noticed how beautiful the flowers are looking when I walked past the potato field the other day," Suzzanne says.

"No, not perfect looking. Like *actually perfect.* They have stamens and pistils in the same flower. They have everything they need in themselves."

"Is that unusual?" I ask.

"It's not so much that it's unusual; it just goes to show that plant gender is not black and white, just like humans."

"So you're saying that all nightshades are nonbinary?" Suzzanne asks.

"In a way. I guess it depends how you define *nonbinary.* Like whether it's containing both or actually being *neither.*"

"You're nonbinary, right?" I ask Mands.

They nod. "But my dudes, potatoes, the nightshades, they're *everything,*" Mands says, totally alight with energy. "They're like nonbinary, bisexual—or pansexual, really. Or maybe, actually, they're aromantic? Because they don't actually need another plant to pollinate. They self-pollinate. It's just so cool."

"Maybe we're all just potatoes," Suzzanne muses, and I feel both intrigued by this conversation and a little too old for it. Mostly, I'm jealous of Mands's and Suzzanne's ease when it comes to talking about the fluidity of both gender and sexuality. I wish I knew all of this when I was their age and had friends to casually talk to about it.

I really could've used more discussion partners. Though I've only ever been in relationships with straight men and I know I present as a totally straight woman, I'm not one. Or not *totally*. What do I desire? I turned that part of me off so long ago that it's hard for me to even remember. But listening to these two talk so openly about all of this has me wanting to interrogate.

What I desire isn't limited to gender. What I want is a feeling. What I want is someone as invested as I am. What I want is warmth and softness but also intensity. Tender electricity. Everything that has become vacant in my marriage.

I've felt that feeling before with women, even if my encounters were brief and mostly drunken and maybe not quite full-on sex but something close to it. They were all so long ago, but flashes of those moments come back to me sometimes. I remember kissing a college classmate in a bathroom stall at a bar. I remember a woman I met at a party in New York, before Jared. How we made eyes at each other the whole night and found out we lived in the same neighborhood and shared a taxi. How the minute we got in the cab, we were all over each other. My apartment was the first stop, and she didn't get out with me. I never saw her again.

What excites me about these memories is not so much who they were with but how *alive* I felt at the time. How eager I felt. How free.

"Earth to Paige!" Suzzanne shouts at me.

I snap to. I don't know how long I have been standing by a wooden rack not doing anything.

"You OK? It gets so hot in here. We're basically in a gigantic plastic raincoat. The heat can get to you if you're not used to it. Do you need some water or something?" Suzzanne asks.

"Oh, I'm fine, just daydreaming."

Her phone buzzes. Mands's phone too.

"What are those alarms for?"

"It means the workday is done. Frankie insists we all set them so we know when to wrap up, so no one works more than they're supposed to," Suzzanne says.

"But Frankie is still out there?" I ask as we leave the greenhouse. It's hard to believe how cool it feels even though it's eighty degrees outside.

"Yeah, she never stops working," Suzzanne says solemnly. "She's always telling us to do as she says and not as she does. If we all stayed until everything was crossed off the list, none of us would ever go home."

I look at my watch. I don't have to pick Bobby up for another two hours. Maybe I'll stay and help Frankie. After all, what's better than two hands?

"Thanks for coming today," Frankie tells me when I find her. "We couldn't have done it without you."

"Yes, you totally could have, but you're welcome."

"OK, yes, we could have done it without you, but then who would we have gotten to laugh at?"

I can tell this is a joke and I smile.

"But in all seriousness, you make a good team member, Paige."

I do love when she says my name.

"I really liked being here," I say. "It's cool to see you doing your thing. And your crew—Suzzanne is really something, and Mands is just so on top of everything."

"And they both care so much about farming. It's rare these days."

"You're a great role model for both of them." Am I flirting? No, I'm just stating the truth: Frankie is dedicated to her work and is clearly good at what she does.

OK, I'm not *not* flirting.

Because Frankie is hot. And it's not just her tattoos and muscles. She's magnetic and confident, funny and serious at the same time. She is bighearted. And she is exactly who she is. Her Carhartt wardrobe isn't ironic but actually functional. She wears a trucker hat sincerely. A trucker hat that she told me was given to her by the small organic seed company she's been loyal to for years even though they're more expensive than their bigger, sleeker competitor. She's loyal. She is, I realize, both electric and tender.

"I try to be a good example." Frankie is gathering up tools. "My dream would be for people like them to stick around for as long as possible and take everything they learn here to start their own farms. Have their own crews and everything."

For someone saying something so wholesome and sincere, she looks remarkably sad. "What's wrong?" I ask her.

"Nothing, everything is fine. Or, well, not really. But it will be."

"OK, you don't have to tell me, but I am all ears if you want."

She looks up at me, makes a face like she just tasted something sour. It would be cute if she didn't look so worried. "It's just that this farm means so much to them. It's a queer-friendly space, and people who work here usually come to figure themselves out, you know? Like figure out who they are and what they're made of. And they meet each other. Bond. We're just a bunch of weirdos who want to grow vegetables and joke around all day. And these relationships can carry them into whatever comes next."

I've never felt anything remotely as moving as this about my work. "Frankie, I don't hear a problem here."

"It's just . . ." She trails off. I don't try to fill the quiet. I just look at her. "It's just," she starts again, "that it's becoming harder than ever to keep it all going. I'm nearly out of money. And if it were just me, then whatever, but it's not just me. It's all of them."

"But the line at the farmers' market was practically around the block."

"Well, if popularity alone could pay, then we'd all be doing great. But every single year our expenses get higher, and the cost of living here gets higher too. I increase our prices a tiny bit annually, but I really can't fathom charging any more for what we grow."

"That makes sense."

"I want everyone who works for me to be paid well. To be able to afford to live near where they work and have a good, happy life on a farmer's salary. But that gets less and less possible with every rich city person who moves to Sungold."

I don't say anything.

"Sorry, I didn't mean you."

"No offense taken, seriously." She's not wrong, and I know it.

"It's not even that simple. It's all just a big catch-22. The pricier our area becomes, the more customers we get at the market, especially customers who don't really care how much their vegetables cost. But with those people come higher rent and taxes and all of that."

I follow her to the next garlic row. "So why don't you just charge more? Especially if it's for people who don't care what it costs. And yes, I mean people like me."

"Then the people who grow the food can't afford to buy it. And that just feels wrong. I think it *is* wrong."

It's clear she's been thinking about this for a while. I open my mouth to respond, and she jumps in before I even say anything.

"I'm not looking for a solution. I guess I just needed to say it out loud. Thanks for your ear. I'll figure it out eventually. I always find a way."

I push down my instinct to head right into a brainstorming session. "Thanks for telling me."

"Yeah, I'm good, really, don't worry about me."

"I'm not worried. You seem like you can do and fix just about anything." I think about her with my tire, how easily it came to her. Like she's used to saving the day all of the time.

My phone buzzes. My assistant.

Hey Paige—I know you're OOO, but GMA's producer isn't responding. Details are in your email. Can you call her? Already asked the others.

"I should get going. I'm supposed to be on a sabbatical from work, but it looks like they need something."

"Oh, I didn't know you worked."

She doesn't sound judgmental, but it stings to know she assumed I was a rich city person who could just flit up here for a summer without any responsibilities.

"I run publicity at Wilmington Books, a publishing company. We mainly do self-help books, like ones about how to improve your life. But I'm taking a couple months off while I figure out *my* life," I tell her, searching her face for a reaction.

"How's the figuring out going?"

"I'm, um—let's say I'm figuring out how to figure it out."

She smiles, and that makes me smile.

"Wait." Frankie looks down at her hands. "Does publicity mean you know about social media?"

"For better or worse."

"Mands and everyone keep hounding me about how we need to have a 'digital presence.'" She makes air quotes as she says this.

"Yeah, I mean, the first thing that I do, or that so many people do these days when they discover a new business they care about, is follow it on social media. You could attract a whole new audience too."

"They think it would be a chance to show customers what goes on here, how much we put into the vegetables they love. Maybe sell some Two Peas hats to fund some of the equipment on their wish list."

She looks so bashful telling me this. I'm desperate to

dive in but try to keep in mind she just specifically said no to solutions. "Oh yeah, I heard about a thing for the garlic."

"Yeah, the undercutter."

"It really does sound like a video game villain."

Frankie laughs. "Yeah, Mands is determined to drag me into the twenty-first century."

"Is it annoying if I agree with them?"

"But if we did all the things Mands thinks we need to—I just imagine my dad nonstop rolling over in his grave."

"This was his farm?"

"Yeah, and his dad's before that. I'm third generation. And they're both gone. It's just me now. No siblings. No other family."

It occurs to me we have been talking for at least ten minutes now, just standing in the garlic field. I don't know when we stopped walking the rows. "So is it that doing things how your family did them is a way to keep you close to them?"

"Well, yeah." Frankie looks a little stupefied.

She seems surprised that I was able to sum up so much so succinctly. But that's basically my job. Figure out the point quickly, say it clearly, make it resonate.

I seize the moment. "If you want any help with social media or publicity this summer, I'd be happy to help. It'd be a nice distraction for me, from figuring out my personal stuff, I mean." I do not add that it would also be an excuse to spend more time with Frankie. Whose bandana I want to fold into a square and use to gently wipe the sweat accumulating on her forehead.

"That's a really nice offer."

"It'd be my pleasure."

"I'll think about it."

The look on her face tells me that she's not just saying that. It tells me she'll actually consider it.

When my phone rings, I'm on the couch, wrapped in a towel after one of the longest showers of my life, during which I unsuccessfully attempted to de-garlic myself. I look at the screen, and my stomach turns.

"Hi, Jared," I say warily as soon as I pick up. "Bobby isn't home from camp yet, but we can FaceTime later if you want."

"Actually, I called to talk to you. How are you?"

"I'm fine." I feel caught off guard by his simple question. I don't remember the last time he asked me that. I know he can be kind, it's just that there's often an ulterior motive lurking underneath.

"How's life upstate? Catching lots of fireflies?"

"It's all really nice. I've actually befriended a vegetable farmer, and I got to spend some time today helping with the annual garlic harvest."

"Wow, Paige, that's not a sentence I would've ever expected to hear you say. I thought you'd be upset if you couldn't find a Pilates studio there. I would have never banked on you doing actual manual labor." His tone isn't actually mean, just genuinely surprised. I close my eyes and shake my head, a gesture he can't see through the phone. Sometimes I feel so profoundly misunderstood by him. I grew up in Idaho, for heaven's sake. I know how to be outside in the dirt. Granted, the me that Jared knows is so far removed from where I was raised. Jared knows the me that already moved across the country, knuckled and elbowed my way into publishing, homed in on a capsule wardrobe, and figured out my exact martini order (gin, extra dry, lemon twist).

"Yeah, it's nice to be outside doing something useful."

"So I just wanted to let you know I bought Bobby new roller skates, and I'm having them FedExed to you. The package needs a signature, so you'll need to be there when it comes first thing tomorrow."

"Jared, Bobby doesn't need new roller skates. The ones he has are totally fine."

"On the phone the other day, he said his ankle was sore. I bet because his skates are too tight. Plus these are the best of the best—top of the line."

I pick at a thread at the hem of the towel. "If you were listening, you would know Bobby's ankle was sore because he tripped at camp. He told you that." The way this man thinks he knows what's best and just swoops in with *things* when no one asks for them.

"What happened to just being grateful? Just please be home for the truck."

"I have plans tomorrow morning." Sure, my plans are to go grocery shopping and to buy a new handheld vacuum. But they're still *my* plans.

"Where do you need to be, Paige? Picking garlic?"

I look down at my hand that's not holding my phone and see that I've made a fist without realizing it. My chest feels tight. "We talked about this. Where I am and what

I do with my time this summer is none of your business. Just like I don't need to know what happens on your sailing trips."

"Fine, whatever, bye, Paige." He says it in one breath and hangs up the phone.

I pick up the hard, scratchy pillow next to me, press my face into it, and scream. Then I realize that, for the first time in my adult life, I'm not sharing a wall with a neighbor. I lose the pillow. I scream until my throat hurts.

VI

FRANKIE

It's only ten in the morning, and it's already ninety degrees. The air feels thick and heavy. Though I wish I could just jump into a swimming hole, I tuck my pants into my socks and my long sleeves into a pair of disposable gloves. I'm headed to the zucchini. I'd rather be too hot than totally scratched up by the plants' prickly leaves and stems.

Our zucchini crop is thriving this year. The stalks are thick and hollow, like gigantic straws, and the squash erupt at their bases. I use a small, sharp knife to cut the zucchini off the plants, being sure to leave a little bit of stem on each one. I place them in five-gallon buckets as I go.

"Wait!" Mands shouts at me. "Stop walking, let me get this shot!"

They aim their phone to take a picture of me carrying a bucket in each hand. "Can you hold them up higher?" I lift them. Begrudgingly. "Smile!"

"Do I have to?" I'm not even joking. Each bucket weighs at least twenty pounds, and I'm not particularly in the mood to cheese right now. Being yanked out of my workflow to make "content" is killing me.

I quickly smile for Mands's camera, then immediately resume walking.

"Wait, sorry, my thumb is in this photo. Can we do this just one more time?"

I grunt. Actually grunt. And then I lift the buckets again and smile a little maniacally.

"It's blurry." They hold up their phone to show me the photo as I pass. In addition to being blurry, it's also completely backlit.

I take a deep breath. "Mands, I appreciate your efforts here, but I think you're way better at farming than you are at whatever this is."

"So that offer to help with social media stuff—did it have an expiration date?" It's been a little over a week since Paige mentioned helping me, and I'm finally calling her.

"The offer stands. Happy to help. You might have to get a cell phone, though, if you decide to start posting. Which also means you could just text me instead of calling me on the phone like it's the eighties."

"You know what's nice about talking on the phone? All of this banter. Try that over text."

"Frankie, texting is all banter. I hate to be the one to tell you this, but you sound like our grandparents."

Is Paige flirting? Would I be able to interpret that over text? "All right, I'll add 'consider a cell phone' to my list. Anyway, are you free for dinner one night this week? I could cook in exchange for your thoughts."

"Sure. But I think I'm getting the better end of the deal."

"I don't know about that. Oh, and Bobby is welcome to come too."

"You know, it would be nice to have dinner with an actual adult conversation," Paige says with a laugh.

OK, *that's* flirting. I can feel the heat of it in my cheeks.

"Actually, do you know anyone who babysits? Maybe someone from your crew? I haven't been away from Bobby since we got here, except for when he's at camp."

"Hold on, let me get my address book."

"An actual address book?"

"Don't sound so surprised."

I give Paige Suzzanne's number, as I know she does some nannying in the winter and has a younger brother she pretty much raised.

One of the greatest parts of being a vegetable farmer is trading with my market friends. I always put aside stuff for the other vendors and end up leaving with loaves of bread, pints of berries, sometimes a beeswax candle or a jar of honey. Our behind-the-scenes bartering feels like a big old *fuck you* to the way modern capitalism works.

I pack my van with my haul, including a dozen eggs from Yolko Ono Farms and a whole bird from Peep This Poultry. I am grateful for the drop in temperature predicted for this evening. I'll be able to roast a chicken without heating up the entire house.

When Paige knocks on my door a few hours later, she looks so different than she did at the farm for the garlic harvest. She's in wide-leg jeans and a tiny, tight white T-shirt. Did she blow-dry her hair? It's so shiny. She's wearing loafers. The stack of bracelets on her wrist makes a pleasing jingle when she moves her arm.

I look at her. Really look at her. I can't tell if she's wearing makeup or not, but her skin looks especially glowy. I take in the tiny moments of her face. How did I not notice that scar above her eyebrow before? She's so beautiful that I can't help but smile. There's also something different about her that I can't quite place. Not in her appearance, but in her energy. Like she's wound up tight. She's clutching a bottle of wine as if it were a life jacket in a storm.

"Hey, how about I open that? And you go keep Fran company?" I gesture toward the couch.

As she passes me, I can smell her perfume. It reminds me of the fancy candles that Abby is obsessed with.

"How's the best girl in the world?" I hear Paige mumble to Fran as I step into the kitchen. When I join her, I pass her a glass of wine and set a bowl of green olives on the ottoman. I take a sip from my own glass.

She looks straight at me and takes a big gulp. "Is this a date?"

I grin. And I realize what's different about her. She's nervous. "Do you want it to be a date?"

"I'm not sure, do you?"

I wait a moment.

I take a breath.

I consider it.

Dating isn't something I do. I hook up. I don't spend time talking and *feeling*, let alone integrating someone into my life or figuring out how to do the same in theirs. But seeing Paige be so sweet with Fran, and her already knowing Fran before she came over tonight, feels nice. It feels cozy. Close. I don't hate it. And I don't hate the idea of this being a date. Of getting to know Paige more. But I have no idea how she's feeling.

"Look, Paige, I promise I didn't ask for your help with social media just to try to get you to my house for a date."

"Oh, OK."

I can't tell if she's relieved or disappointed. It seems more like the latter. "But I'm also really happy you're at my house."

She bites her lip. "I am really happy to be here."

If Paige wants to put that on the table, I'm game. I feel my cheeks flush.

My kitchen timer dings. "Come with me," I say.

Paige follows me into the kitchen, and I give her a loaf of bread, a board, and a knife. I pull the roasting dish from the oven, and I'm delighted to see that the chicken is perfect. Browned all over, the skin crisp like a potato chip. The carrots and onions around it have collapsed into a jammy heap. While the chicken rests, I shake the jar of vinaigrette I threw together earlier with the fresh garlic, which is milder than garlic that's been allowed to cure, and spoon some over lettuce I already washed and tore. I put halved cherry tomatoes on top of the greens and use a vegetable peeler to shave aged Gouda over it all. I carve the chicken and put it on a platter alongside the roasted vegetables. I spoon what's left of the dressing onto the chicken. I place both the salad and the chicken on the small table in the kitchen that I already set with dishes and cloth napkins.

It's not *not* a date. And looking at the table I set, I admit to myself that I probably knew that before.

Before Paige takes a seat, I tell her to wait. I tear off a piece of bread. I drag it through the bottom of the roasting dish, letting it soak up the chicken fat and little bits of sweet onion.

"Come here," I tell her. "The best bite in the world."

I hold up the piece of bread.

She looks me straight in the eyes as she opens her mouth.

I feed her the bread.

She closes her eyes and nods appreciatively.

"Frankie, that is so fucking good."

"I know."

So . . . it's a date.

While we eat, we manage to actually talk about social media. Paige scrolls through the profile Mands set up, tapping at the screen with a deftness that is completely foreign to me. What I feel watching her with a smartphone is probably what she feels watching me use any tool on the farm.

"So what do you think?" I finally ask.

"It's good. The captions are really funny. But can I be brutally honest?"

"Always, please."

"The humor is great. I don't think you should lose it, but I think you're missing something by being *just* funny. Having spent only a little time at Two Peas, the specialness of it all doesn't come through here."

I nod. "You're right. But how? What would make that come through?"

Paige enthusiastically rolls off a list of ideas: short videos of farming projects, crew interviews, on-the-street interviews at the market with our regulars, photos of the communal lunches, weekly recipes. When she says we should emphasize my natural charisma and calls me the heart of the operation, I'm as flattered as I am overwhelmed. I don't even know where to start. "It sounds like a lot to manage."

"How about I help you, then? I really like hanging out at the farm, and Bobby's in camp all day. I could use a project that isn't *me*. We could try it for, like, a week and just see how it goes?"

"I do think seeing you more sounds really nice," I tell her, and she blushes. "Let's try it out. But Paige, I want to be upfront about money. I have no idea what anyone charges—"

"Frankie, money didn't even occur to me. You're giving me something productive to focus on."

"OK, as long as we're on the same page."

"We are."

"Hey, can I see your profile?" I ask her. I'm so curious what she puts out to the world. Paige presses more buttons and hands me her phone.

Her most recent photos are of places around here. The view from Route 53. An ice cream cone at Lakeside. The gigantic catalpa tree on the road that leads to the farm. There are some pictures of Bobby, but none where you can really see his face. All of the shots look bright and beautiful, like life through rose-colored glasses. But they also leave out so much.

"Now can I be brutally honest?"

"Always, please," she replies.

"Everything just looks so . . . so . . . perfect. But that's not what life is actually like. Yours, mine, anybody's."

"You just described social media." She laughs like I have some kind of effect on her, and I join her.

I lift my wine. "Well, cheers to the mess that's just outside the frame of every photo."

We clink our glasses. We eat our meal slowly, but Paige eats with gusto. She shares stories the same way. I learn more about her job, the authors she works with, the books she's excited about and why she's excited about them. I hear how she got to New York from Idaho because she was following her big sister, Eve. How she loves the city but sometimes finds it overwhelming. How she misses the big sky. I learn that she was captain of her high school's soccer team and prom queen too. I find out that she's always wanted to be a parent. That even though stuff in her marriage hasn't been ideal, she wouldn't change a thing because it would mean not having Bobby. That her relationship with her sister has always made her want for Bobby to have a sibling, but her sister's kids have kind of taken up that role. She asks good questions too: "Did your dad create any traditions that you still do even though he's not here anymore?" and "Did he have any nicknames for you?" and "What about your mom?" and "When do you miss your dad most?"

I tell her about Harvest Feast in the fall, the big dinner my dad started for the crew a week after our huge

Thanksgiving market. The way it let him say thank you without words. I tell her that Frankie is my nickname, that my dad knew from an early age that Francesca was just too girly for me. I tell her that my mom left when I was just a baby. I tell her that I miss my dad most when I feel alone in the business, when I wish I could ask him a question.

"What would you ask?"

"If he's OK with me updating some things."

"And what do you think he would say?"

I deepen my voice so it sounds like his: "I trust you, kiddo."

She reaches over for my hand and squeezes it gently.

It's maybe my best date.

I consider her, really consider her again. "He'd like you."

"What makes you say that?"

"Because you're curious. He liked people who wanted to understand things."

We wash the dishes together without talking, the silence companionable, then return to the couch and sit with Fran between us.

Paige looks at me. I look at her. Neither of us says anything for what's probably about ten seconds, but it feels like an eternity.

I am trying to read the expression on her face, but I can't decipher it.

If she wasn't interested, she would've already left, right?

If she wasn't interested, she'd be on her way to get Bobby.

If she wasn't interested, she wouldn't have gotten so quiet when I suggested we move to the couch.

And then, like a splash of ice-cold water to my face, it

dawns on me that if I wasn't interested, I wouldn't be so concerned about whether or not she was interested.

"So you and Bobby's dad—"

"Not an issue."

She's interested.

"But you're married?"

"Yes, but this summer is a trial separation. Things haven't been good between us for a while, and I'm here seeing what it's like to be on my own with Bobby."

"And?"

"And I'm realizing there's a lot more I want."

She stares at me, and it feels like perhaps I'm part of what she wants. The thought makes me feel warm. I stare right back at her.

"Can I ask you something else?" I force eye contact with her.

"Always, please." She holds my gaze.

"Are you into women? Have you ever even kissed a woman? There's no wrong answer. I'm just curious."

"Yes. More than one. A long time ago, but yes."

"And?"

"And what?"

"Did you like it?"

"Yes." Then after a moment, she adds, "A lot."

I feel my pulse speed up. I feel excitement rising inside of my chest like seltzer bubbles. "What would you like right now?"

"What would you like?" she responds.

I answer wordlessly. I put my hand on her leg and look down at it. I see my rough hand curve around her knee as if I'm claiming it. I grip it not so much with urgency but with intention.

She rests her hand on mine. I like the way they look together. Hers is softer and so much paler than mine, since she hasn't worked outside every single day for years. She takes a breath and weaves her fingers between mine. I curl my fingers so hers have no choice but to clench more tightly.

I tilt my head to face her. "Paige," I say, my voice measured.

She looks up from our hands without loosening her grip. "Yes?" I watch her swallow a gulp of nerves.

The air feels thick, our tension filling the narrow space between us like humidity, unseeable but palpable. Sticky.

"Can I kiss you?" I ask her.

She doesn't answer me. She just leans forward and presses her mouth against mine. I feel her smile as we kiss. I smile, too, but also feel something below my smile. Something heartier. Something more substantial.

I move one of my thumbs up and down against her cheek, like I need to be closer to her even though our lips are already touching. How could we possibly be closer? But I know a way. I take her bottom lip between my own and hold it there for just a moment, and she lets out the softest groan I've ever heard. Her mouth opens, and our kissing becomes animalistic, like if we could swallow each other, we would. We sigh into each other, like two cats purring. But the self-assured way she shows me what she wants isn't like a kitten. It's more like a lion. I suspect she can roar. All I can think about is how much I want to hear it.

After a few minutes, Paige stands up, faces me, and looks down at my lap. "Can I sit here?"

I nod. This is *happening*.

She straddles me, a leg on either side of my own. Her body on mine fits perfectly, like a softball resting in a mitt. I wrap my hands around her hips. I hold her firmly. She gently places her hands on my face. She looks at me as if she's studying my features for an exam she'll have to take later.

"How'd you chip that tooth?"

"I was a senior in high school and decided I'd try to skateboard," I tell her. "I was trying to impress a girl."

"And did it work?"

"The skateboarding or the girl?"

She laughs.

"In the end, neither panned out."

She leans in to kiss me, but I stop her. "My turn. How'd you get that scar?" I touch the spot just above her eyebrow.

"My sister pushed me into a coffee table when I was a kid."

"How did the coffee table fare?"

She smiles. She puts her hands back on my face. "You're so beautiful," she says.

I feel my cheeks get warm. No one ever calls me beautiful. Hot, maybe. Sometimes even handsome. But not beautiful.

Because I don't know what to say, I close my eyes. She leans in and kisses each of my eyelids, and it is perhaps the most tender thing anyone has ever done to me in my whole life. Each press of her lips feels like reassurance, like a small weighted blanket on each eye.

She glances at the clock on the wall. "I should get going. I told Suzzanne I'd be home by nine." She stands up and walks toward the door. I'm right behind her.

"It's supposed to rain tomorrow, so I'm taking Bobby to the roller-skating rink after camp. Do you want to maybe come with us? It could be fun! Or weird. I don't know. I just want to see you."

"It's a date."

I walk her to her car. The night air is cool. I can see all of the stars. "Well—"

"—Well," she says at the exact same time. We beam at each other. There's a giddiness in the air.

Her face turns more serious. "Thanks for such a nice evening."

She gets into her car, starts it, and then rolls down the window. "Frankie?" I walk a little closer, put one hand on the roof, and bend down so my face is right in front of hers.

She undoes her seat belt and leans forward and kisses me. A short burst of a kiss. An "I had to do that once more" kiss. She shifts back, puts her seat belt on, and closes her window, not saying a word but grinning ear to ear. As I walk back to my door, I realize that I am grinning too.

I pour cream in my coffee and dial Abby's number. She picks up on the first ring.

"I kissed someone I probably shouldn't have," I blurt out.

"Someone on your crew?"

"No! I would never! You know that."

"OK, so if it's not someone who works for you, why is it someone you shouldn't have kissed? Are you related somehow?"

"Jesus, Abs."

"Ohhh. Did you finally kiss Paige?"

"All right, calm down," I say preemptively.

"I think you should be elated. *I* am. She's hot, and she likes you."

"I shouldn't have kissed her. Because I am seeing her again today. With Bobby." I'm staring out the window overlooking all of Two Peas, in hopes that this will ground me.

"I'm sorry, what's the issue?"

"Well, you know, it means I might have to, you know, like . . ."

"Acknowledge it? Talk about it? Get to know her? See her more than once? Develop and navigate feelings for another woman?"

"Yeah. All of that," I grumble.

"And would that be so bad?" Abby puts her phone on speaker, and I hear her chopping something.

"Well, it definitely could get confusing. And I don't have time for confusing." Abby never gives me a hard time about the fact that I'm a grown adult who has never been in an actual romantic, long-term relationship.

"I don't know, Frank, maybe it's not that it's confusing but that you getting to know someone might mean they would get to know you too. And that can be scary. It would also be a change, and I know you don't like things to change."

"OK, whatever." Even though I started it, I'm ready for this little chat to end. Abby loves therapy and feelings and what she calls "processing." "So how do I get out of roller-skating?" I know I sound exasperated.

"You don't. You go and be nervous and awkward and enjoy that flutter." A beat passes. "How was the kiss?"

"Nice . . . good . . . yeah, it was nice," I say, though I'm sure Abby can tell I'm downplaying it. The kiss, the *kissing*, wasn't nice or good. It was perfect. Charged and intense but also sweet.

"Frank, my dear friend, I have something to tell you that I know you'll find devastating but is actually totally normal and very human."

"Yes?" My patience is thinning. Has thinned.

"You have a bona fide crush on a hot mom."

"Gross."

"It's not an illness, Frank. It's a crush. Most people enjoy them. Try to enjoy it."

Abby is right. I know this, but I'm not quite ready to acknowledge it. "Well, it's been illuminating as always to talk to you," I say.

"Love you too." I hear the sound of dishes crashing in the background. "I gotta go handle this," she says as she hangs up.

VII

PAIGE

The local roller-skating rink isn't the reason I chose Sungold, but it's definitely a perk. Especially on a rainy summer day like today. The rink is pure small-town charm: a squat, single-story building with a huge neon sign outside that's partially broken so it just blinks *ATE!* Inside, the air smells like old socks and fresh popcorn. Speakers are blasting '80s classics, and arcade games blink on the far side of the space. Banners hang on the walls commemorating each year the local roller derby team took home the state championship.

It's surreal to be here with both Frankie and Bobby. I usually keep the various parts of my life disconnected. Work. Bobby. Shit with Jared. I guess there aren't really that many other segments, unless talking on the phone with my sister counts. But I couldn't fathom waiting longer to see Frankie after our kiss last night. If it means already mixing whatever is between us with my time with Bobby, so be it. I like that life here feels less regimented.

Besides, I didn't go to Frankie's house *planning* to kiss her. I went to talk about how I could help her out. But did

I wear my best bra? Take care to put on fragrance? Did it occur to me that I was flustered when I got to her door? Did I think about kissing her while she fed me bread with her hands? Duh, duh, duh, and duh.

There's just something about her. Something remarkably undramatic and straightforward and dedicated—to her farm and to her community. I feel like a teenager around her, which is especially nice, since so much of my life feels so full of adulting. But I don't just feel happy around her; I also feel turned on. Which, while a little unexpected, is delightful.

Bobby and I have been skating happily ahead of her when we hear the boom, and I turn to see Frankie sitting on the ground.

"Are you OK?" I shout as I glide toward her. Bobby follows after me.

Maybe inviting her here was a bad idea? What if she's broken something and can't carry crates or dig holes or whatever it is she has to do next at the farm?

"I'm fine!" she yells over the sound system. I offer her my hand, but she waves it away and turns on all fours to press herself back up to standing. The three of us gather in a huddle. I don't want to keep skating until I know she's OK.

"Are you sure? Did you hurt anything?"

Frankie laughs. "Sometimes it really pays to be fat. If I was bony like you, I might have a broken tailbone right now."

"Frankie!" Bobby yells. "Don't say bad words."

"I didn't say a bad word."

"Yes you did," he insists. "You said *fat*."

I wince. I've tried my best to keep diet-y stuff out of my son's life, but it's a place where Jared and I really diverge. We're both genetically thin, and Jared's been an athlete his entire life. He's never been made fun of for his body. Or catcalled. He's never understood what it's like to live in a body that's constantly scrutinized. In turn, he does a lot of scrutinizing of other people's bodies. He judges them, ranks them, and compares himself to them. As he sees it, there are good bodies, and there are bad bodies. And I know I'm complicit when it comes to weight too. I've often lamented when an old piece of clothing no longer fits within earshot of Bobby. Even though it's irrational to expect that my favorite sweatshirt from high school would still hang the same baggy way decades later.

Now dozens of moments like this flash through my head, and I wish I had steered Bobby differently, because I see now that Bobby telling Frankie that *fat* is a bad word feels like he's telling her that *she* is bad. I am mortified. Not because of him, but because what he's saying reveals blind spots in my parenting. Before I can jump in and clear the air, Frankie responds.

"Bobby, *fat* is not a bad word." She says it more calmly than I ever could.

"It's not?"

I watch her soften her already soft gaze at him. "No, it's just a word that describes the size of something. It's not an insult. I'm fat, just like you're eight and have brown hair."

"But I thought I wasn't supposed to call anyone fat?"

"Well, it's probably not ideal to go around commenting

on anyone's body, no matter what size they are." She's handling this moment so comfortably that I am in awe of her. Her easygoingness is definitely attractive.

Bobby makes a face as if the math in his head isn't adding up. "But Frankie, you called my mom *bony*."

She laughs. "You're absolutely right. I probably shouldn't have said that. I'm fat, and I'm also imperfect."

"I knew I was right!" He smiles proudly and pushes off, gliding across the shiny wooden floor. He pumps his arms to propel himself forward, and soon it looks like he's a duck on water: smooth, controlled, fast.

Frankie and I lean against the railing and watch him. "You know what this place needs?" I say, waving at the rink. "Theme nights. Like Roller Disco or a Queer Night. Or they could project movies like *Hairspray* and *Whip It* over on that wall. Or maybe—" I could keep going, but Frankie is shaking her head at me.

"What?" I ask.

"I just love the way your brain works."

I blush.

"Hey, do you want anything?" I nod toward the concession stand.

She shrugs like she could go either way. "Do you?"

I don't have words for what I want right now. What I want is to kiss her again. What I *really* want is for her to momentarily make everything else in my life evaporate. To wave a wand and vanish my responsibilities. I want to know what her body looks like under all those layers. I want to know what her hair smells like. I want her to tear my clothes off. I want her to tell me exactly what to do. I want her strong hands on me.

But I can't say any of that. So I just move slightly closer to her on the railing so I can feel her side against mine. "Yeah, maybe a drink or a snack or something?"

She shrugs. "Everything is a little overpriced here."

"Oh, it's on me!" I quickly stammer, abruptly aware that the cost didn't even occur to me.

I didn't grow up with the kind of money that Jared and I live with. And sometimes I'm almost embarrassed at how oblivious I've become to the cost of things. But Frankie lives in the real world. She's pragmatic. I was raised like that. My parents scoff at how much we spend on Bobby's private school and his nanny. When they visit, I make sure to buy all the groceries we'll need before they come, lest they see the prices in the stores where I shop.

Being with Frankie makes me feel like I'm a little closer to the ground. Being with her makes me remember what it's like to pause before pacifying whatever I'm feeling—hungry, thirsty, lonely—with a *thing*.

"Want to split a Coke and some fries?" I ask her.

"That sounds perfect, actually."

She finds us a Formica-topped table along the perimeter, I get our order, and we take turns dipping the fries in mayonnaise and ketchup while we continue to watch Bobby.

"He's really good," Frankie says.

"I know, I love watching him skate. It's so peaceful. I taught him how, but he's far surpassed my abilities."

"Really? That's amazing. It clearly lights him up. He is so in his element here. It's so great that you support it."

I feel the compliment in my bones. It's not just the parenting acknowledgment; it's the feeling of standing next to someone who sees a part of what makes my kid special and thinks it's worth celebrating, not questioning.

She turns her head to look at me. "Hey, I'm sorry I called you bony."

"It's OK. I am." I smile, thinking about what I'm about to tell her. "And for whatever it's worth, I like your size."

"You do?"

"How could I not like that there's a lot of you?"

She smiles wide, and it's so joyful that I wish I could somehow put the feeling in a locket and wear it on a chain around my neck and never take it off. I wish I could touch it whenever I needed to remember the look on her face right now and the warmth I feel knowing I helped produce it.

"Will you help me skate?" she asks. I haven't known Frankie for long, but I know that asking for help is not something she does often or easily. With this question, this admission of need, I feel something invisible shift between us. Like a seesaw that has righted itself, the weight of it all just balanced.

"I'd love nothing more," I tell her.

We get back in the rink. I turn to face her and extend my arms, palms up. "Hold my hands. I'll skate backward and you can lean on me."

She takes my hands and wobbles a bit, and she grimaces. But I am not swayed. I know she can do this. I squeeze her fingers for reassurance. We make it halfway around the rink like this, and I still sense Frankie's shakiness. "How are you feeling?" I ask her as we turn a corner.

"Nervous."

"I've got you." And for the first time since we started our loop, she looks up at me, not down at her skates. We keep going, and soon I feel her unsteadiness give way to something more trusting.

"That's it!" I'm trying not to sound too excited, but I can't keep a little enthusiasm out of my voice.

We do another two laps like this, our hands clasped the entire time, me going in reverse, her eyes on mine. We don't say a word. We just skate. It feels so nice to be the one who can literally support her. A sweetness spreads through me, pooling in my stomach. I like getting to offer this to her.

After our next go-around, she tells me she's ready for a break. We pull over and watch Bobby as he weaves in and out of other skaters and practices going backward. At one point he tumbles, falls to the ground, and quickly gets back up.

"He's just so fearless," Frankie says.

"I have no idea where he gets that from."

"Are you serious?"

I look at her and pinch my eyebrows together, a question mark.

"*You* are fearless."

"Me?" It's not how I think of myself. I am a schedule maker. An anticipator. A person who soothes her nerves with spreadsheets. I love a meal plan.

"Yeah, you picked up your life and moved to the middle

of nowhere to figure out what you want. Also? You're a really fucking good roller skater. Which I'm learning takes a lot of guts." She says this all so earnestly that I have no choice but to take it in. To accept it.

I reach for her hand and squeeze it. "I like the way you see me."

"I like seeing you."

VIII

FRANKIE

I am shivering in blasting air-conditioning in the Sungold Credit Union office, learning about loan options. Brenda, my friend from high school, happens to be a loan officer here and is doing her best to explain various programs to me. Words like *interest*, *amortization*, *debt allocation*, and *repayment* ricochet around the room like paper airplanes.

While I'm accustomed to nature's unpredictability impacting a growing season, I'm not used to the level of financial uncertainty we're in right now. And it feels extra scary because I don't have my dad or anyone else to rely on. This is all on my shoulders.

"I can answer any questions you have, and if I don't know the answer, I'll get it for you," Brenda says. My eyes glaze over, and I see a picture of her son on her desk. He's the same age as Bobby. Paige mentioned that the two boys have become friends at camp.

"How's Eric doing?"

"He's fine, thanks for asking. But don't use Eric to avoid this conversation." I'm quickly learning that Work Brenda is very direct.

"I'm just overwhelmed." I clasp my hands tightly in my lap like I'm preparing for bad news.

"That's normal. Why don't you take these materials home and just read everything, and you can come back next week and we can talk more about it all?"

I nod, then gather the pamphlets and tuck them under my arm.

"We'll figure something out," Brenda reassures me. It feels good to hear even if I'm not sure I want to go down the loan road with all of its paperwork and indebtedness. There's also the grant that Mands keeps pestering me about. No matter what, something has to happen. We're not going to make it on just our market sales.

"Oh, Frankie!" she says as I'm halfway out the door. "See you at the fair tonight? With Abby and Paige and Bobby? He and Eric have really hit it off."

I smile and nod, but my shoulders tense. I can't decide how I feel about a public group outing with Paige. It's not something I've done with anyone I've kissed before.

"Isn't Paige so great?" Brenda asks.

I can't tell if she knows that there's something going on between me and Paige, if she's fishing. "She sure is" is all I say.

Once we're all in line for the Ferris wheel, Bobby and Eric beg to ride together. Abby looks at Brenda. "I haven't caught up with you in so long, Bren. Why don't we pair up?"

Abby turns in my direction and raises her brows. In our younger days, she would have stuck her tongue out at me.

"Looks like that leaves me and you?" I say to Paige.

We pile into our compartments, and then I'm headed to the highest point in Sungold with Paige's hand in mine.

"So you told Abby?" Paige asks. Her tone is breezy, but I'm not sure if it matches her feelings.

"Yeah. I did. I tell Abby just about everything. Sorry I didn't ask you first."

"No, it's OK. I don't know, I kind of like the idea of you calling your best friend to tell her we kissed. It's cute."

I exhale. "I didn't know if you wanted to keep things a secret or something. Because . . . your husband."

She pivots her body toward me so one knee knocks mine. "Look, Frankie, I know us kissing while I'm . . . *married* is . . . well, I don't know exactly what to say. I know it is not ideal. But Jared and I have been done for a while. I've known that, and I do think, deep down, he knows that too. What I haven't known is how to get out of it."

She clears her throat and locks eyes with mine. "That's why I'm here in Sungold. But I'm here on this Ferris wheel because I like you."

"I like you too." It shouldn't feel like such a big thing to say this to her—"I like you"—but it's new for me, to express an emotional desire for a woman I'm interested in and not just a physical one. I grip her hand more tightly.

Paige drops her head to my shoulder. "I won't pretend getting out of my marriage will be seamless. But I know I want out."

I feel myself turning red.

"I didn't come here looking for anything like this." She looks up at me and gestures in the air between us. "I'm surprised by what's happening. And *happy* about it. But I know I come with a lot of baggage, that's all I'm trying to say. But I guess that's what it is to date in your forties. Not that we're dating . . . are we dating? I feel like I can't stop talking." She begins to turn red too. "Can you say something now?"

"I guess now is when I admit that I've never really dated before." I feel my face get even redder. "I don't really have actual relationship experience. Not that we're in a relationship!" We both giggle. "So yes, you have baggage, but I also have a pretty notable lack of experience. I usually just, like, hook up with people who are stopping through town."

"So you're a fuckboy?" Paige's smile turns sly.

"I wouldn't say *that*. I would say I have a really busy life that includes sex, but not, you know, dating."

"Are you saying you just want to fuck me?" Paige unlaces her fingers from mine.

"No!" I nearly yelp. "That's not what I'm trying to say at all."

"So you *don't* want to have sex with me?"

"No, I do! I really do."

She laughs. "Good. I want to have sex with you."

My whole body grins at that.

"But I also want more than that," I say. The words surprise even me. I am articulating this as much to her as I am to myself. But saying the words out loud to Paige doesn't feel like I'm trying them on. It feels like they fit.

Because I don't just want to have sex with her. I want more. I want her to keep showing up at the farm. I want to go to the roller rink again with her and Bobby. I want to hear how sexy she sounds when she gets strict and tells

Bobby to be careful. I want to eat ice cream with her and take her to Sam's and sit at the bar. I want to shoot the shit together with the bartender. I want to put my hand on her back when I laugh at something funny she says. When she gets up from her stool to go to the bathroom, I want her to kiss me in front of everyone. I want the men around us to be jealous. I want her to sleep in my old T-shirts.

I want all of this because I like how I feel when I'm around her. I like how her energy and curiosity are infectious. I like that being with her makes me more reflective. I like that being with her makes me feel brave. How seeing her literally pick up her life and go somewhere else makes change seem less threatening.

"OK, my turn to ask you something." Paige reaches for my hand again and makes circles on my palm with her thumb.

"Anything."

"Because I've just learned you're extremely experienced and have kissed lots of girls . . ."

I roll my eyes at this, affectionately.

"But do you agree that the other night, that kiss was like—"

"Spectacular?"

"Yeah, I thought so too."

I lean forward and kiss her. Short and sweet. Tender and new.

"I have so many things I want to ask you." Paige looks at me, her eyes shining.

"Like?"

She sits up taller and takes a breath. "I want to know

when you got Fran. I want to know why you've never left Sungold, and I'm curious if you ever want to. I want to know if you ever wanted kids, not because I think everyone should; it's just that you're really sweet with Bobby. Like you know how to speak his language, meet him at his level. I want to know how you learned to cook. I want to know more about your dad. I want to know your favorite vegetable to grow and your favorite one to eat, and I am desperate to know if they're the same or different."

"You had those all locked and loaded?"

She laughs. "I just want to know you, Frankie. I think you're special."

Before I have a chance to answer any of her questions, the Ferris wheel jerks to a stop, and we're back at the bottom. We could've just stayed on the ground for all I know. I've been so present with Paige that I never even paused to take in the view.

The next day, Paige shows up to the farm bright and early.

"I have a plan," she says as she approaches me in the pumpkin field. She pulls out a piece of paper. It looks like notes from someone who is trying to solve a murder. There are big titles like "goals" and "tactics" circled in red pen, small notes like "giveaways?" and "AMAs?" (whatever that means), along with lines drawn in thick marker connecting everything.

"OK, I'm going to suggest it's best for me to not try to decrypt that and just trust you."

"That works for me." Paige winks. She's loving this, isn't she?

The sincerity with which she's helping Two Peas isn't lost on me, though. She's clearly spent time thinking through this. Thinking through how to support the business. How to support me.

"I was about to go check on everyone to go over the rest of today's task list, but I could spare five minutes first if you need to talk through anything."

"Five minutes?" Paige lifts one eyebrow. Without saying anything, she walks toward the shed, and I follow her. Before the door is all the way closed, she's all over me. Her hands are wrapped around the nape of my neck, and she's on her tiptoes to press her mouth to mine. Her kiss is enthusiastic, energetic. It feels so good to be this wanted. Affirming. Especially because I want her just as much.

My right hand slides to her waist without a conscious thought, and my left goes to her head and closes around her soft ponytail to draw her closer. After a moment, she pulls back. "Sorry, I have just been really wanting to kiss you again. Like properly. Not like a 'quick, is-anyone-looking-at-us' peck on the Ferris wheel."

"I've wanted that too." I step back and feel the loss of proximity acutely. "As much as I'd like to be in two places at once, I have to get back to the crew."

"No, absolutely. And I really did come here to work."

"Whatever you say, boss." I give her a snarky thumbs-up.

"I think today, just ignore me. I was hoping to just follow you and the crew around a bit. Maybe get a little video of you all just doing your thing. How does that sound? I'll only stay until lunch."

"That all sounds great except the ignoring you part. I don't think I'll be able to do that."

She laughs. "Yeah, I guess it is unfair. I have a sanctioned reason to literally stare at you as long as I want, and you have to pretend I'm not here."

She follows me out to the fields and walks just a little too close, like she's taunting me. I explain to the crew what she'll be doing this week. "I'm willing to give it a shot," I announce to everyone.

They all respond with some version of "Finally!"

Mands, Suzzanne, everyone else, and I start trellising peppers, each of us taking a row and working the string carefully but quickly around the plants. Paige points her phone at us, at *me*, and snaps away. It feels strange to have someone pay this kind of attention to what I am doing. Like I'm the draw, not the vegetables. I feel uncomfortable. Like I want it all to just be how it's always been, where the work can just speak for itself. But behind Paige's camera is Paige herself. Looking at me like what I am doing is fascinating. Looking like she believes in me. Feeling her gaze helps me remember that I can believe in me too.

IX

PAIGE

After spending almost a week at Two Peas, I've gotten into the farm's daily rhythms and gotten to know the right moments to sneak away with Frankie.

She and I said we were coming into the shed to get seltzers for everyone, but now we are kissing, her back pressed against the door. We just finished filming three videos, and her whole crew is outside on their lunch break. The only thing that separates us is this weather-battered wooden door.

Our kissing has moved from casual to fervent. Frankie pauses and lets out a low growl, like the guttural equivalent of "Yes, more of this." She puts her hands in my hair, and even though my eyes are already shut, I somehow close them even more. It's like my eyeballs roll back in my head at the sensation.

I pull away a little, trying to catch my breath. "Frankie."

"Yes?" She's almost panting.

"I want so badly to keep going, but everyone . . ." I gesture behind her. "And I need to go get Bobby. Can we pick this up again soon?"

"Yes, anytime. Literally anytime."

I smooth my hair and take a deep breath in an effort to get some of the color to mellow on my cheeks. We step back outside.

"Paige, stay for lunch!" Mands points to what really does look like a perfect BLT, piled high with Two Peas tomatoes and crunchy iceberg lettuce, which Frankie told me she grows specifically for this purpose.

"I wish I could. I'll take one for the road though."

As Frankie wraps a sandwich in a paper towel, my phone rings. I see Brenda's name flash on my screen. "Hey, is everything OK?" I say as soon as I pick up. She's hosting Bobby for a playdate with Eric, and I have a vision of a broken arm or projectile vomiting.

"Everything is great! The boys are having so much fun, and Eric was begging for Bobby to stay for dinner and sleep over—I told him I had to call you first."

"Oh! Of course, that's great, as long as you're sure?"

Brenda assures me she's happy to have him and get them both to camp in the morning.

"I'll come by and drop off pajamas and clothes for him."

"Honestly, don't worry about it," Brenda says. "He can borrow stuff from Eric. They're the exact same size."

I get Bobby on the phone just long enough to tell him to behave and that I love him. I head back to the picnic table. I don't know that I've ever smiled this wide. Frankie's brows are raised.

"Change of plans. Bobby's spending the night at Eric's."

"Does that mean you can stay and help us weed the carrot field?" Mands interjects.

"Sure! That sounds fun."

"It isn't, but we do it together, so that part is fun," Mands says.

Frankie winks at me.

Soon we are all on our hands and knees pulling tiny weeds from around the carrot plants and stuffing them into five-gallon buckets that fill painfully slowly. It's tedious work.

"I am not trying to complain," I whisper to Frankie when we're close to each other. "And I know I have no idea what I'm talking about, but is this really the best way to do this? It feels so endless."

"It's not the fastest way, but it's the most thorough." She sighs, and I stay quiet, sensing she's figuring out how to express what she's thinking. "My dad swore by hand-weeding, by using all no-till methods."

Right. This is not just about the weeds. It's about tradition. And grief. And change. "I know this is a naive question, but what does 'no-till' mean?"

"It means disturbing the soil as little as possible to keep it as healthy as possible."

"Are there other ways to help the soil besides crawling around like we're all looking for a lost earring?" I'm not trying to criticize her method. I know I don't know anything about farming. But I do know about time management. "I'm just looking around at all of these talented people and wondering if this is the best use of their time."

She pauses, sits back on her heels, and rests her hands on her thighs. She surveys the field. She observes her crew inching down the rows. "You're right."

I am surprised. My eyes go wide. "I am?"

"I mean, yes and no. Who's to say what's the best use of anyone's time? But you're saying what Mands has been saying for years now. But you're more objective. There are a lot of ways to do things. Maybe we don't have to be *so* meticulous."

"Hey."

She looks at me.

"Your attention to detail is a beautiful thing." There's more emotion in my voice than makes sense for a conversation about weeds.

She smiles.

"Maybe there's a way to do both? Maybe there's a way to hold on to some of the old-school stuff but also incorporate some new-school stuff?"

"So just . . . school?" she says.

We both laugh.

She nods as if she's taking this in, as if she's letting the conversation rewire a few things inside of her. Then her voice gets serious. "So if Bobby is having a sleepover . . ." Her eyes narrow, and her grin becomes catlike. "Would *you* like to have a sleepover?"

My entire body tingles.

"As long as Fran's OK with that."

"I'm sure she'd love to see you."

A few hours later, Frankie's crew has left for the day, and we're turning the weeding buckets upside down so they don't fill with rainwater. We're both covered in dirt and sweat. Frankie reaches her hand out to grab mine and we walk that way, holding on to one another, all the way to her house. We're both quiet. I feel like I'm full of helium, like if she lets go, I might float away.

When we get inside, Fran trots over to me. I kneel down to pet her, and she turns over and shows me her belly.

"Oh, someone is *very* happy to see you," Frankie says. "Actually, how about you two hang out for a bit while I take a quick bath? I'm filthy. If you want, you can use the shower in the other room."

I stand up and face her. "Can I watch?" I express this desire before I fully process it. I don't want her to leave my side, even if it's just to bathe. Plus, I don't just want to see her naked. I want to see her get naked.

"Watch what?"

"You."

"You want to watch me take a bath?"

"Yes." I'm already picturing her stepping out of her clothes and revealing the parts of her that aren't streaked in mud. The parts of her I haven't gotten to see yet.

"No one has ever watched me take a bath before."

I stay quiet.

"OK," she says, and I hear a little excitement in her voice. "Sure, yeah." It seems like she's tickled by my request but also maybe a little turned on too. I know I am.

I follow her to her bathroom. She puts the stopper in the drain of her enormous clawfoot tub and turns on the taps, adjusting them until steam comes off the water. "I like it really hot."

"Me too." It's a silly joke, but I can't resist.

She doesn't laugh, though. Her taking me and my words seriously ups the tension in the small space. This is for real. She just points to a small stool next to the sink. "You can sit there." I like her telling me what to do.

We both get very quiet while Frankie unbuttons her shirt. We lock eyes as it falls off her shoulders. Her jeans come off next, and she stands before me in a tank top, underwear, and socks. I see the tattoos on her thighs for the first time and get a better view of the ones I've glimpsed on her forearms that go all the way up to her shoulders.

I want to study these tattoos, become an expert in them. I want to be able to sketch them from memory. There's lots of nature and words too. I see the letters B-I-L-L in a heart with the years marking her dad's birth and his death. There's evidence of her life all over her. Her thighs are thick. Her legs are so strong they almost look like they're made of marble, like two sculpted columns.

The fewer clothes she has on, the more self-assured Frankie seems. It's as if in watching me watch her undress herself, we're sharing a mutual understanding of my attraction. I'm watching and loving it, and she is loving that I love it.

She puts one hand on the edge of the sink basin to balance herself and uses the other to remove her socks. Then she places both hands at the hem of her tank top and lifts it up and over her head, and she does the same with her plain sports bra. Finally, her underwear goes too.

I am so grateful I am already sitting down.

She's unlike anyone I've ever gotten to witness naked.

Looking at her is like simultaneously seeing the curves and softness in a Botticelli painting combined with the strength and solidity of a football player. Her stomach and breasts are so full and round. If I were to draw her, there would not be a single straight line. She is so distinctly herself. She is moreish. She is so fucking beautiful.

I say no words, but I know my body language is communicating everything I'm feeling. My eyes feel like they've gotten bigger. I bite my lower lip. I lean in.

And then she turns around, and her back is to me. The tattoos from the front of her thighs wrap around to the back of them. There are tangled flower vines and foxes and rabbits. Looking at her is like being outside. Her ass is substantial and mesmerizing. I want to know what it feels like to lie on it, to rest my head on it, to grip it with my hands and kiss it. I want to use my body to tell her body how much I want her.

She steps into the bath and gently lowers herself down. I am jealous of the tub. Oh to be the thing Frankie settles into, the thing that gets to wrap itself around her.

The water quickly turns her pale skin bright red. Her breasts floating on the surface are the most sublime sight I've ever seen. She bends her knees, and her stomach rests against them. It looks as soft as bread dough, and as tender.

She wets her washcloth and adds soap to it from the bottle on the shelf next to the tub. She turns it into lather and bathes herself. As she does, neither of us says anything. I have to remind myself to breathe. These are, I am sure, the most erotically charged minutes of my life.

Of course I want to touch her. Of course I want to feel her

touch me. But just watching her in the bathtub—watching her while she watches me watch her—is something beyond touch. The tension in the air is so thick it feels like our hands are already on each other.

But when I look down at my own hands in my lap, I remember just how filthy I am after spending the whole afternoon weeding.

I stand up from my stool, and though I don't want to be anywhere but here, I need to shower before we go any further. Before I can't help but reach for her skin. And I could use a minute alone to wrap my head around what's about to happen. Because it's clear what's already started. And while it feels absolutely like what I want, I want a moment to confirm that with myself.

"I am going to take the fastest shower in the world. Can you stay right here? Like please do not go anywhere?"

She laughs. "I'll be waiting."

X

FRANKIE

I steep in the water for another couple of minutes and feel how excited I am. I tap my heart, willing it to beat a little slower. *There's no rush*, I remind myself.

Paige returns from the shower wrapped in a towel. She is wordless. So am I.

I pull the plug from the drain and stand up, revealing my entire body to her. Even though she's covered, the desire I see in her eyes makes me feel like we're both stripped down.

There was a time in my life when I wouldn't have wanted anyone to see me naked, especially a thin woman I was attracted to. That has thankfully changed over the years, and now, *right now*, I feel so comfortable in my body. I understand why she wants it. Because in front of her, with her eyes on me, I feel formidable.

I know I'm a lot to take in, so I let her. I pause for longer than I need to before stepping out onto the bath mat. I grab a bath sheet from the hook on the back of the door and wrap it around myself. Her stare is like a spotlight trained directly on me.

"Follow me," I say. They're the first words either of us

has spoken in what feels like an eternity. The silence has built so much tension. Before she can respond, I turn and open the second bathroom door, the one that leads to my bedroom.

It's pitch black, but I want to see Paige just as she has seen me. I turn on the lamp on my nightstand, and its glow is warm. I sit on the edge of my bed, and she stands in front of me.

She drops her towel. We're both quiet again. Now she's naked and I'm covered, but the dance is the same. Now I get to watch her just like she watched me.

Paige's size and shape are no surprise—she's normally in spandex at the farm—but her nakedness softens her somehow. Most of her clothing is just so ironed and crisp, so professional looking. Even those workout clothes look like they have some kind of built-in scaffolding, some compression to make her body more rigid. But here, with nothing on, there's a suppleness about her. I think of softly whipped cream. Of cashmere. Of ripe fruit.

I pull her closer to me and drop my head to kiss her neck and inhale the faint smell of sunblock lingering under soap, as if she didn't quite scrub the entire day away. As if she couldn't wait to get out of the shower so she could be exactly where she is right now. I get lost in the dips between her shoulders and her neck, the bones of her clavicle firm under my lips.

While I've enjoyed the anticipation of sex before, I've never experienced it quite like this. I'm usually responding to tension that's been built over hours, not weeks. I'm usually feeling the bubbliness of urgency, the thrill of knowing something is about to happen that will end just as quickly as it started. It always feels almost a little bit illicit, since it's so ephemeral.

But right now, I'm with Paige, who knows so much about me already. Who knows everyone's name at Two Peas. Whose son I've shared french fries with. It feels different. It feels charged and consequential. It feels scary in a way I'm not used to but also special in a way I'm not used to. It makes me want to move slowly. Deliberately.

I move my mouth farther down and plant short, brief kisses on each of her breasts. She pushes herself even closer to me and puts her hands on the sides of my head and holds me firmly against her chest.

I take this as an invitation, as instruction. I close my eyes and open my mouth around one of her nipples, and she sighs. I move my tongue in slow circles, and she moans. I do the same on the other side, and she presses into me even more, so much so that I start to fall back on the bed, my towel coming undone as I do.

She climbs on top of me, laying the full weight of her body on mine. "Is this OK?" she asks.

"Fuck yes," I answer.

We kiss like we haven't before. She's not just on me. She's pinning me down. We grab at each other, and it's as if a door has opened into a room neither of us was sure the other was ready to enter. There's excitement in the air, but there's also tacit permission.

She pulls her face back from mine and rolls over to lie beside me, facing me. I turn on my side toward her. "I've wanted you since the beginning," she says.

"You mean, since that day you waited in that long line, then didn't want to buy anything?"

She laughs, and it cuts the tension, makes me feel lighthearted.

"It's not that I didn't want to buy anything. I was just overwhelmed."

"By how hot I am?" I smile.

"Yes, I saw you, and then my brain stopped working." She rolls her eyes, teasing me. But then her expression goes more serious. "Actually, I'm sure I wanted you then, but I didn't know it yet."

"When did you know?"

"I think I started to know when you changed my tire. I couldn't get over watching how your body moved. And those forearms." She reaches out and strokes one admiringly.

"My forearms?"

"Yes, I've learned, from you, that I have a thing for forearms. And then later when we made those tomato sandwiches and I was sitting with the crew for the first time, I noticed your tooth. I was just staring at it and wondering how you chipped it, and I wanted to know everything about it, which made me realize I wanted to know everything about you. It was like a portal or something. And then I realized I liked it because I got to see it when you smile, and I love seeing you smile. It makes me want to smile. And I . . . I don't know. I just like being with you. And I just wanted to be as close to your tooth and your mouth as I could be." She closes her eyes and pulls away slightly.

"Paige."

She opens one eye and squints at me. "Sorry I just said all of that. It's embarrassing."

"Don't be embarrassed. It makes me happy to know that. I've wanted you for a long time too."

She props herself up on an elbow, looking like she doesn't believe it.

"Really?"

"Paige." I run a finger down her hip. "I assume you know that from the way I kiss you, but if it helps to hear it spelled out, let me try. I clocked you the second you set foot in front of me at the market. You are incredibly beautiful, of course. But also you seemed funny. When you forgot to take your vegetables and everything, our whole exchange just made me laugh. It stayed with me. The more time we've spent together, the more time I want. You're smart. And willing to try new things. And you're so good with Bobby. You're so loving. The crew loves you. I don't know . . . you've . . . you've surprised me. This has all surprised me."

She smiles. "Frankie, I want you so much. But I'm . . . I'm nervous." She looks at the ceiling, and I can tell it's hard for her to say that.

"Does it help to know that I am too?"

"You've done this before."

"Not with you."

She smiles bigger. She is so, so gorgeous. I rest my hand on her hip. "What do you want? How can I make you feel good?"

"I want you to fuck me," Paige says.

I raise my eyebrows. I'm a little taken aback. I imagined

she'd be more shy with me. "How do you want me to fuck you?"

"I don't know . . . the normal way?"

"There's no such thing in queer sex."

She laughs. "OK, OK, but you know what I mean . . ."

"Paige, I want to know *exactly* what you want. Nothing would be hotter for me than to be able to give it to you."

She looks like a deer in headlights. I am getting the sense that it's not that she's keeping anything from me. It's more that she's not actually sure what she wants. I squeeze her hip gently, as if to emphasize the question I'm about to pose. "Forget how we get there. How do you want to feel?"

She softens her face, then closes her eyes. "I want to feel like I'm somewhere else, somewhere only you know. I want you to take me somewhere, then bring me back down to earth." She opens both eyes. "I want to feel out of my body but totally in my body? Does that make sense?"

It doesn't totally make sense, and yet, it does.

I nod. "I get it. Is there anything off-limits? Anything that would make you feel unsafe?"

"No one has ever asked me that."

"I'm sorry this is an exception." I press my hand into her back, in hopes that it's steadying.

"But no, nothing is off-limits. You can do anything you want."

I grin. "OK, and it's fine if you change your mind."

"OK, well, what about you? Is there anything off-limits for you?"

"You want to fuck me?" I thought she'd only be interested

in receiving, at least during our first time together. I'm realizing, though, that was just an assumption. I'm also realizing that I'm assuming there will be more times than just this night.

"Yes. I really want to." She nods, simple and direct, no hesitation.

I clear my throat. "I'd really like that."

"So? Anything I should know?" Her gaze searches my face.

"No, nothing is off-limits for me, but I guess I wouldn't like to get on top of you because I don't want to crush you." I laugh a little.

"I can handle more than you think I can." She smiles at me coyly.

"Is that a challenge?"

"If you want it to be." She reaches over to me to push my towel all the way open. Her fingers graze my shoulder, and she slowly trails her hand down my side all the way to my thigh, as far as she can reach. Her touch feels curious, like she's trying to memorize the topography of my body. "Frankie, I think I don't want to talk anymore."

If we were in a movie, this is when the song would take over the dialogue. Our bodies begin to express things that words don't have the capacity for. Like how we want so badly to know each other beyond our biographies. Like how much we want to experience each other in a way our chemistry allows only the two of us to feel. Like how greedy we are for each other.

I move my hand from her hip up the length of her body, following the curve of her waist all the way up to her neck, moving to just my fingertips at the tiny patch of soft skin behind her ear. I trace her knowing that I will be able to touch her again, but this will be the only time I'll ever do it for the first time. I run my hand back down to her waist. I move my entire self farther down the bed.

She uses both of her hands to push herself back against my pillows, and I kneel in front of her. She seems eager for more than light touching. I meet her urgency with deliberate slowness. I slowly stroke each of her legs. I hold her feet in my hands and squeeze them gently.

She bends her knees. I run my hands up her legs and push them open slightly, revealing her to me. I lick my lips. She slides her feet farther apart to give me access, and I can sense how badly she wants me to touch her, to fuck her.

I don't.

I move slowly. I tease her.

I run my fingertips along the inside of her thighs and lie down between her legs, making myself comfortable.

I start to kiss all the places I'm touching, replacing my hands with my mouth.

As I get closer to where she wants me, I slow down even more. I nuzzle my nose into her handful of soft hair, swaying right and left.

She places her hands on my head and bucks her hips. She's insisting, pleading with me to do more.

Finally, I do.

I glide my hands underneath her thighs and hook my hands around her legs. I grab her firmly and pull her closer to my mouth. She lets out a gasp.

I use my tongue to work closer to her, laying it flat and

firmly against her clit. She digs her fingers into my head. I take this as confirmation that I'm exactly where she wants me.

I lick her, over and over and over and over, until I start to lose myself in it. While eye contact is sexy, getting to be buried in her allows me to feel so unbelievably present. I can smell her and taste her and feel how she responds to every single thing I do. With nothing between her and my mouth, I'm able to act as voracious as I feel. Her grip gets tighter and tighter, like a vise. I can feel her nails in my scalp.

"Frankie." Her voice pierces the room.

I stop and look up at her, nervous that maybe this is too intense for her.

"Too fast?"

"No."

"Too much?"

"No, no . . ."

"Are you OK?"

"Yes, I am so OK." She takes a breath, she's nearly panting. "I just need you inside of me."

I smile. I love that she's telling me.

"Now." Her voice is authoritative and desperate at the same time.

I stare at her while I lift my hand to my mouth and slide two fingers past my lips. I make them slick. She stares at me like she cannot believe what she's seeing. I revel in her stare.

I keep looking at her as I dip one finger inside of her and then, quickly, add the other. She is so wet and so open and so ready. I push inside of her, and she lets her head fall back as she moans. I take my time fucking her, going more slowly than I think she wants.

"Harder. Please."

I stop with the teasing. We're here now. I add a third finger. She pushes against me as if to say *There, right there.* I speed up and press even more deeply inside of her with each push. Her moaning gets louder and more rhythmic. I can tell she's building. She squeezes my fingers tightly, and I push even more.

And when I sense she's getting close, I dip my head back down and lick her while I fuck her. I move my free hand to her hip and grip it tightly to give me as much purchase as I can find.

"Fuuuck." She yells, and I feel her whole body tense. She thrusts her hips up and down, amplifying everything I'm doing with my fingers inside of her and my mouth outside of her.

"I'm going to come. I'm about to come."

I already know this. But I like hearing it anyway.

As she comes, she screams. She clenches my fingers inside of her so hard that they hurt. And then everything goes quiet and all of that tightness, all of that tension—it turns to silk.

I keep my fingers inside of her for a few moments and revel in how wet she is. I remove them so slowly it's like a tease in reverse, a slow goodbye.

I make my way up the bed alongside her. Her eyes are closed. I don't push her to say or do anything. I offer her silence.

Paige turns to face me, opens her eyes wide, and smiles. "Wow. That was . . . that was . . . you are so good at that?"

"Are you asking me or telling me?"

She laughs. "No, I am telling you that you are so good at that."

I smile at her, her perfect face with that scar above her brow.

She smiles back and starts laughing a little bit.

"What's so funny?" I ask.

"Nothing! I don't know why I am laughing. I think I am just happy. This is . . . fun?"

"I'm definitely having fun. We're having sex. Sex is fun."

"It's fun with you."

"Sex is funny, isn't it? Like, when you zoom out, it's just a couple of adults trying to make each other feel good. When I think about it that way, it just feels like a playground. It can include so much."

"Such as?" Paige's eyes brighten.

"Like . . . anything. Whatever makes you feel good. I like when sex feels expansive, when it's about enjoyment and feeling connected, not just in service of, you know, only getting off."

"I hear you, but when you just made me feel the way I did, I would not mind just doing that over and over."

I laugh. "But I can make you feel more things, and I bet you can make me feel a lot of things too. You have already." I'm aware of how wet I already am, even though she hasn't touched me.

"I want to do all of the things with you." There's a big smile on her face. And hearing her say this makes me feel like we're both eager for this to not just be a one-time thing. That we want to try to do so many things with, and *to*, each other.

"Can I do everything to you that you just did to me?" she asks.

I arch my eyebrows. I nod. The mood gets more serious.

She kisses her way down my body, and I can feel her excitement as she reaches my waist. She looks up at me, pauses, and grins. I move one of my legs to the side to open up space for her and to silently tell her that I'm ready when she is.

She traces the tattoos on my thighs with her fingertips and kisses each one. I close my eyes and enjoy the sensation of her exploration. She moves her fingers from the tops of my thighs to the inside of them, and her touch goes from feeling exploratory to more deliberate. More intense.

I grab a firm pillow from behind me and slip it under my lower back to prop me up so that she can reach me more easily and I don't have to hold myself up. She casts her gaze down and slowly slides one finger into me. She closes her eyes and smiles. I know the feeling she is having, the distinct satisfaction of feeling just how ready I am for her.

"More," I say.

She looks up at me and stares while she adds another finger.

She looks excited. She looks like she's getting to do something she's long wanted to do.

She begins to move her fingers in and nearly out of me, and I push myself into her.

She bends her head down and starts to kiss my thighs

while she fucks me. She moves her head closer to where her fingers are.

"Can I?" she says.

"Fuck yes."

She takes her fingers out of me and replaces them with her tongue.

As she goes down on me, she becomes less shy, and I let go more too. I bury my hands in her hair. I tell her how good it all feels. She works her mouth on me hungrily and puts both of her hands on my stomach. At first she touches it gently and then more insistently. I put my hands on top of hers and squeeze them to show her that she can touch me even harder. I can tell that she likes how much of me there is, how there's so much to grab and hold and feel and claw.

Our bodies are so different, and just as I'm drawn to hers, she's drawn to mine. When I was younger, I thought my differentness—my bigness—was something disappointing. I've learned over the years that it's the opposite. I am not disappointed in my body. I like how I feel in it. I walk around the world taking up space, being noticed when I enter a room. If I had to describe myself, I'd say I'm a house. It's safe here. It's sturdy. And inside, it's warm and there's so much softness.

Sometimes when I'm having sex with someone, I think, *You are lucky to have all of this.* It's true, but it's also self-protective. It's a thought that acts as armor, to shield me from the way I was conditioned to think of my fatness. With Paige, though, my ego is quiet. I know I'm not just some fascinating form for her to explore. I'm what she desires. Witnessing her discover my body makes me feel wanted. It makes me feel sexy.

She lifts her head up from me, and her fingers continue to work fast and deep. "Every part of you is so fucking hot," she says, and then she immediately puts her mouth back on me, eagerly. I know she isn't saying this to gas me up, or to even get a response. She's just thinking out loud. She's in the moment.

I relax into her, and my mind goes wonderfully blank. I am thinking of nothing except how good she is making me feel. How effervescent. Everything in me is coiling tighter and tighter. I feel like a champagne cork being eased from its bottle. A gentle build at first, and then the pressure is so much that I am expanding into the edges of my body and can't help but erupt outside of it. I come in her mouth.

Paige holds her tongue on me until my breathing slows to normal. She lifts herself up, smiles at me, and gently lies back down, resting her cheek on my stomach.

She wipes her mouth on her hand. She licks her lips. "You taste so good."

"So do you," I say.

She props herself up and gives me a look I can't read.

"Frankie, I hate to say this. But I am . . . well, I am . . ."

"What?"

She takes a deep breath. "I am so hungry." She starts laughing. "Do you have anything to eat?"

"A woman after my own heart."

I grab my robe and tie it tightly. I reach into my drawer

for a clean flannel and toss it to her. “Put this on and come with me.”

She stands up from the bed, throws my shirt over her shoulders, and buttons it as she follows me.

I look back at her with a grin and prop one hand on the wall to steady myself. “I’m going to make you the best spaghetti of your life.”

“I think I just came again,” she says. We laugh our way into my kitchen.

XI

PAIGE

I roll my windows down on the drive home from Frankie's house. My hair is still damp from her shower. My speakers are on full blast. My heart is beating fast while I replay everything that happened last night, and again this morning.

Brenda texts that camp drop-off went well, and it's like my whole body smiles. I get inside my house, lie on the couch, and take a moment to enjoy the quiet. I want to let the time that only Frankie and I know what happened between us last a little bit longer before I call my sister.

"Eve, are you sitting down?"

"No . . . should I be? What's wrong? Is Bobby OK? Are you OK?"

"Oh my god, no, sorry, everything is fine. I just have something I want to tell you, and you might be surprised when you hear it." I am practically breaking into song.

"You sound . . . excited?"

"I am. And, OK, a little freaked out. But in a good way."

"Spill."

"I slept with someone."

"I'm sorry . . . you what?"

I close my eyes. "I had sex with someone. Not Jared."

"Yeah, I figured. So who is he?"

"She's named Frankie."

"Oh! Ohhhhhh."

Eve knows I haven't been with anyone but Jared since he and I have been together, even though he has strayed and, at various points, I've been tempted. Eve also knows that before Jared, I rarely slept with anyone, even those I took more seriously—and even more rarely had experiences with women. It's a part of myself we haven't talked about in ages.

"Well?"

I almost laugh at how eager she sounds. "It was fucking amazing, Eve. I don't know what it means or where it's going, if it's going anywhere, or what. But I know I want to do it again."

"Fuck, I'm jealous. Sex with someone new, when it's good, is so thrilling. Not to shade Brian, but it's just not exactly surprising anymore. So tell me. About this Frankie. Who is she? What's she like? Is it true that sex with a woman is so much better?"

"I'll answer in reverse order because I know you want me to."

She cackles.

"I don't know about women *in general*, but yes, sleeping with Frankie was incredible. Just, like, so connected and intense, but also playful. And there was so much communication? Which sounds basic, I know, but, *wow*, does that make a difference for me. And it was only our first time? I can't imagine it getting better, but it's so exciting to know it could. I just love her body so much. I'm drawn to it. Like when she was doing stuff to me, it was so good, but I just really, really—" *Can I tell her this?* I ask myself.

"Paige," Eve demands.

"I just loved going down on her." All of a sudden I find myself getting shy with the one person I've never, ever been shy with. I take a breath. "I just felt like I was, like, given access to this incredibly special, private thing, and I just could not get enough. Have you ever just wanted to, I don't know, like, *devour* someone?"

"Oh my god, you love her."

"No! I don't *love* her." Heat rushes to my cheeks. "I just really love fucking her." I hear just how defensive I sound, which only makes Eve laugh harder.

"OK, OK, I get it. Wow, so tell me about her. Who is she?"

"She's a farmer. She runs a vegetable farm. I met her on our first day here at the market."

"OK, this is a Hallmark movie. Fancy city girl moves to the country and falls in love with a farmer. Oh my god, does she also grow Christmas trees? Does she have a small bakery in the small town? Did you two get snowed in at her house, and you had to spend the whole weekend together? I know it's July, but still."

"Oh, calm down. But I *did* get a flat tire the other week, right after I met her, and she happened to drive by and helped me fix it."

"Get the fuck out of here." I wish we were in person right now so I could see the look on her face.

"But yeah, we have been spending a lot of time together.

I'm helping her with social media for her farm. She's very analog. She doesn't even have a cell phone, she does all her bookkeeping in an actual notebook, and she insists on doing everything at her farm in the most old-fashioned ways."

I hear Eve take a deep breath, as if she's gearing up to say something she's not sure how to express. "I hate to even bring it up, but how are we feeling about—"

"Jared?" I say it so she doesn't have to. I get up off the couch and pace the living room. I know Eve is waiting for me to continue. But I know I can't take anything back with her once I've said it.

This summer was supposed to be a trial, but somewhere between spending so much time outside at the farm, finding pleasure in keeping this small house tidy and full of meals and clean laundry, and hearing Bobby laugh with his new friends, I've started to feel like myself again. Like the me that Eve grew up with. Happier, looser, more spontaneous, less attached to the trappings of my life in Brooklyn.

I bite my thumbnail and cough lightly, all just to buy a little time before I get up the nerve to say what I'm about to say. "I don't think this separation is just a trial anymore." I feel defiant even though my voice is a little shaky. "And not because I want to run away or anything to do with Frankie. It's just that being here and figuring out a different life—a different way I could live—is bringing me back to myself. I'm remembering who I was before Jared. I miss her. And being here is helping me find my way back to her."

"I miss her too." Eve's voice chokes up. "You know,"

she says, "I can hear her in your voice. The old you. I was thinking that the other day, actually. That talking to you lately has felt like my phone calls when I was in college and you were still in high school."

My whole body relaxes hearing this.

"We'd just gab for hours. You would crack me up with your high school stories. Like how you convinced your entire class to come to school dressed like the principal, down to the plaid scarf she always wore." We both giggle at that memory. "It's like these years with Jared have chipped away at your goofiness. I think being in Sungold is bringing it back. Like you're the Paige who isn't afraid to be a little imperfect or even get in a little trouble."

"I know Jared will not make this easy, but I'll get through it."

"And you won't be alone."

Now I'm the one who is choked up. My phone beeps. "Hold on, I'm getting another call—" I look at my screen and see that it's Frankie. "I'm going to jump off."

"Is it her?"

"Shut up," I say with a laugh.

"Knew it. OK, go! Love you! Talk to your girlfriend! Tell her I say hi!"

I begin to protest that Frankie is *not* my girlfriend, but Eve has already hung up.

I pick up Frankie's call. "Hey," I say. Can she hear my smile?

"Hey. I just wanted to check and see how you were doing. After everything." As if I could forget.

"Fucking great," I say happily.

She chuckles. “Me too.”

“Listen, Bobby is going with Eric and two other kids to the roller-skating rink after camp today. I need to pick them up at five and figure out something to feed them for dinner, but I was thinking maybe I could come later today to document some stuff around the farm, and maybe we could hang out after your crew leaves? Before I pick up the boys?”

“Hmm.” It’s like I can hear her thinking. “Maybe.”

Oh shit. I’m probably coming on too strong. I haven’t dated in a very long time. “It’s fine if that doesn’t work. We just saw each other. I get it, I understand.” I’m rambling but can’t seem to stop. Before I fill with more air, Frankie interrupts me.

“I want to see you.” She says this with a hearty laugh. “I’m just supposed to be getting a compost delivery this afternoon after everyone leaves. I think I need to sign for it.”

“Oh.”

“Yeah, let me just call them and make sure they know where to leave it. It shouldn’t be an issue. And if it’s OK with you, I’d much rather take you out on my canoe than hang out at the farm longer.”

“You have a canoe?”

“Are you actually surprised?”

“You have a point.”

“It’s a date,” she says.

If I thought observing Frankie change my tire was hot, watching her single-handedly get a canoe on top of her pickup truck is really doing something for me. She jostles it into place as if she's been doing this her whole life, which I suspect she has.

"Ready?"

I nod yes.

Being around her at the farm with Mands and Suzzanne and everyone on her crew felt totally normal. We were all joking and laughing together. Suzzanne even let me film her giving a very impassioned speech about how underappreciated kohlrabi is. "People don't know what they're missing! All the crunch of a broccoli stem and so little flavor!" I told her this wasn't as convincing as she seemed to think it was. But then she grabbed a lemon and some salt from the little kitchen area in the shed, peeled a kohlrabi with her pocketknife, cut a bunch of thin slices, squeezed some lemon over them, sprinkled them with salt, and passed them around.

I took a bite. "OK, now *this* is convincing." We redid the video, this time with her sampling her esteemed vegetable, the crunch audible.

But now it's just Frankie and me in her truck. No crew, no distractions. It's the first time we've been alone since I left her house early this morning. I'm nervous, trying to think of what exactly to say. *Last night was fucking amazing, and it's making me rethink every sexual experience I've ever had?* And *I wish I could snap my fingers and just be divorced?* Or maybe *I feel so connected to you, and that's freaking me the fuck out, because what does that even mean?* Or perhaps *Can we fuck right now?*

But before I say anything, she just reaches over the

center console and takes my hand. She gives it a little squeeze. "I'm looking forward to taking you to my favorite spot."

I smile at her and hold her hand and let the wind from the open window wash over me while we drive.

She unties the canoe and slides it off the truck, making the whole thing look like a breeze. After she positions it in the water, she directs me to sit in the seat toward the front. Then she rolls up her pants, throws her boots and socks into her truck, and pushes the canoe, with me in it, into the lake. She carefully steps in, assumes her seat, and picks up the paddle she left at the ready.

The sun is emanating its late-afternoon glow, and the lake looks like liquid gold. I can smell the pine trees around us and the lingering hint of bug spray and sunscreen from the public beach area. I can hear kids splashing and laughing in the background, but each time Frankie puts her paddle in the water, it all gets farther away, like we're leaving the world behind in our gentle wake.

Frankie's paddling is just like her: steady, consistent, strong. She waves and says hello to the other canoers and kayakers we pass. She steers us toward an outcropping of trees that juts into the lake like a protective arm, then slips us around it into a narrow cove. Here, the water is still and glassy, the air quieter, as if the rest of the lake has been muted. It feels like the kind of spot you'd only know about if you grew up here and spent whole summers exploring.

She paddles us all the way to the shore, and then we both get out of the boat and pull it from the water. We turn it upside down so it doesn't go anywhere. Then she takes my hand again. "Come with me."

We walk through the woods, maybe a quarter mile, the canopy above filtering the sunlight into shifting, dappled patches. There's no path, just the gurgle of a narrow stream guiding us forward, its banks soft with moss and fallen leaves. Frankie stays barefoot, maneuvering easily over roots and rocks, as if the forest is an extension of her own backyard. When the trees open up, we step into a clearing where a small swimming hole glimmers, ringed by tree trunks and branches arching overhead. The water catches the light like stained glass, and the hush of the place feels almost reverent—a tiny outdoor chapel.

She promptly takes off all of her clothes and leaves them in a pile next to the water. She jumps in and goes all the way under. She emerges, hair wet, smile enormous. "Come in."

I strip down and heap my things next to hers. I jump in, my toes pointed and my arms over my head. Frankie reaches her arm out under the surface, and I grab it and she pulls me toward her. The water is cool and almost silky. I wrap my arms around her neck and my legs around her body, and I hold on to her. "Am I pulling you down?"

"I'm standing. You're perfect."

I squeeze her even tighter. I press myself against her. I bury my mouth in her neck and kiss the same spot over and over again. I taste her sweat and sunblock and the water too.

"I am so happy you're here with me," she says.

I untangle myself from her and float on my back next to her. "This is so beautiful. Thank you for bringing me."

I plunge my legs back under me and face her, the water pooling between us.

She grazes the lake's surface. "Abby and I discovered it when we were, like, ten. I don't come here as much as I wish I did, but goddamn, it feels so good. It's a little bit of a schlep to get here, but I guess that's why we have the place to ourselves."

"Would you and Abby skinny-dip?"

"Never! I only started doing that when I got older and began coming here by myself. Honestly, being in water totally naked helped me really come to love my body and just feel more at home in it."

She stretches her arms over her head, and I try to picture a Frankie who isn't at ease with herself. "You seem so confident," I tell her. "I can't imagine you not feeling comfortable in your body."

"Well, that's nice to hear. But no, I unfortunately went through the shit most everyone does. Insecurity, all of that stuff. Not to mention that being a fat, gay kid in a small town wasn't the easiest combination."

"How do you feel now?"

"Right now?"

I nod.

"Right now, at this very moment, I feel incredible. My skin feels cool, and my body feels comfortable, and it was definitely fun to watch you get undressed and leap right into the water and not flinch at the temperature."

"Fun like funny or fun like hot?" I raise my brows at her. I'm fishing. Sue me.

"Hot."

I smirk. "Good to know. But how about in general? How do you feel in your body?"

"In general, I guess I'd say *solid*. I feel solid. I feel mostly able to do the things I want to do. I feel grateful. And you? How do you feel in your body?"

"Honestly?" I haven't talked about my body in a long time. Haven't even *thought* about it. She nods at me to continue.

"Most of the time I feel pretty detached from it. I used to feel more *in it*, but then I was pregnant, and my body felt so foreign to me. Some people love being pregnant, and bless them, but that wasn't my experience. And then when Bobby was born, I felt like my body belonged even more to him than to me. He always needed something from it."

"And now?"

"I don't know. I do all of the things I've been conditioned to, like working out and doing endless grooming. But I don't really ever feel *embodied*. I don't think I even really know what that means. Most of the time I just feel like a brain attached with a frayed wire to a physical form I have to tend to."

"How about right now? How do you feel in your body right now?" She inches closer to me in the water.

I close my eyes and check in with myself. I really assess how I'm feeling.

"In it," I say, "totally in it."

I lie on my back and let the water hold me. I close my

eyes and feel the sun's warmth wash over my face. I feel Frankie looking at me. It feels like another way of being held. I let the moment saturate me.

I was still floating when I left Frankie, but picking Bobby and his friends up completely snaps me out of it.

Bobby looks smug, and Eric and the other two boys look like they have been crying.

"Bobby, what's going on?"

"We got into a fight." He shrugs.

"A fight?" I'm shocked. Bobby is eight. He and his friends normally play video games and roller-skate, and they still enjoy the playground. I turn to Eric. "Are you all OK? What happened?"

He's quiet.

"Bobby?"

"It's nothing, Mom. Everything is fine."

Why do I suddenly have a teenager? I put on my most serious Mom Voice. "Tell me what happened. Now."

"I told them how the kids in Brooklyn who roller-skate can do tricks. I don't know why they got so upset."

He's obviously leaving something out. "Bobby—"

"I said that Brooklyn is better than Sungold and Sungold sucks and that no one here is cool." Something about the self-satisfied look on his face feels familiar to me. Then I realize where I've heard this kind of talk before. Jared.

"Eric, boys, can you wait here a second?" I pull Bobby into the hallway nearby. "Listen, I understand if you don't like it here as much as Brooklyn. We can talk about that later, me and you. But you cannot—*will* not—treat your friends like that. It's not kind to put other people down."

"But they're nerds." Bobby wrinkles his nose.

"Bobby, nerds are usually the coolest people in any room they're in. They're so cool that they don't care about being cool. You're a nerd. It's a good thing."

This all seems to shock him a little.

"Whatever." He looks down at his feet.

"Sometimes, when I have the urge to put someone else down, it's because I'm feeling down. If you're upset about being away from Brooklyn, that makes a lot of sense, but it's not an excuse to be mean to anyone."

"I hate it here."

"Which part: the nonstop roller-skating and the ice cream and the fun camp and the new friends?"

He fights a smile.

"Nothing is all bad or all good. It's OK to enjoy some stuff here and still miss Brooklyn."

"I guess that's it." He leans into me.

"We can talk more later, but for now, I need for you to apologize to your friends."

"OK. And then we can get food?"

"I have vegetables in my car from Two Peas I was going to make with pasta. Or maybe a stir-fry?"

"Or we could get burgers?" His voice and eyes are pleading.

I have to admit, a burger does sound really good right now. "Or we could get burgers. If your friends are up for going to Lakeside Cones."

And with that, he runs back over to the bench to say his sorries.

At Lakeside, at a picnic table filled to the brim with boys, I think about how sometimes being a parent feels like a long game of pinball. Your day can be seamless, even a little bubbly. You can feel the nonstick coating of a new romance, the feeling of everything else just rolling off your back, because what could possibly be challenging when you're into someone who is equally into you? And then: *boom.* Your kid forces you to get your head out of the clouds with such abruptness, it's as if you were standing in the park and a dog ran into the back of your knees.

Being with Frankie has me feeling hopeful. Has me feeling like a future without Jared isn't just possible, it's also full of glorious potential. Like maybe I won't just be OK—I might even be happier, more tethered to myself and the people around me. More alive.

Bobby's real-time needs keep me from overromanticizing this shift, though. If I'm going to really date Frankie, really spend time with her, then I'm also going to have to figure out how to make sure it's all OK for Bobby.

"Hey, Mom!" He shouts at me from across the table, ketchup smeared at the corners of his mouth.

"Yeah?"

"Can you ask Frankie if she can take us to see those cows she told us about last time we saw her here? Eric can't believe I've never seen one up close before!"

Hearing Bobby ask to do something with Frankie, completely unprompted, feels like a sign.

He's bouncing in his seat. "Can you text her now?"

I explain to him that Frankie doesn't have a cell phone. "But I'll ask her next time I see her."

"OK, but can that be soon?"

As if I need an excuse.

XII

FRANKIE

It's Monday morning, an hour before the crew is due to work, but Mands came early for coffee. We're glued to the television set in my house, watching the weather forecast grow increasingly ominous. They're on their phone scrolling through updates from a meteorologist they follow.

I take a sip of my coffee and realize it's gone cold while I've been transfixed on the news.

"They're predicting major flooding. It looks like we're going to get two months' worth of rain in one day." Mands runs their hand down their face over and over, a nervous tic I've noticed them do when they're worried about something.

The storm is supposed to hit in a few days, at the end of this week. I've navigated serious weather before, just like my dad did and my grandfather did before him. While we do so much planning and anticipating in farming, the unpredictability of the elements is always a variable. And it's always humbling.

But this forecast is something else. Weather is usually inconvenient at best and a little damaging at worst, but we're not talking about a little damage here. Our land simply can't absorb the amount of rain they're saying we're going to get. We're talking whole crops washed out. We're talking enough water to uproot cabbages and send them bobbing away like beach balls. We're talking about months of work—seeding, planting, cultivating, irrigating, pruning—all swept away overnight.

"Maybe we can get some extra folks in for a bulk harvest over the next few days?" Mands suggests. "Get in everything we can?"

"But what if it ends up not being as bad as they're saying? Then we'll end up picking everything prematurely and be left with nothing for the next few months."

"Boss, it's going to be bad."

"All right. All right." I am aware of what Mands isn't saying, which is "I told you so." I'm aware of how many things they've suggested we do to prepare for something like this and how many times I've vetoed them. Things like digging better drainage around the greenhouse and high tunnels so that our structures don't flood, moving crops to fields on higher ground, diversifying our income streams with things like merch and classes so that we can still earn money even when the farming itself ebbs. But I know we can't go back. It's not the time to acknowledge what we could have done. It's time to figure out what we can do right now.

There's a knock at the door, and I answer it distractedly. It's Paige. I'm happy to see her—I'm always happy to see her—but now really isn't a good time. I tell her Mands and I are working, indicating with my head that Mands is in the other room so Paige knows we aren't alone.

"OK, so I'll be quick." She smooths her ponytail even

though it already seemed smooth. "I know I said I'd do one week of taking photos and videos and everything and we'd see how it all went. And it's already been more than a week, but—"

"Listen, Paige." I'm trying to make my voice as patient as possible. "I really can't talk about social media right now. This storm that's coming in is going to be bad. We have to focus on it. Actually, you and Bobby should probably come stay here. Your house is in a floodplain. You can sleep in the guest room. Plus, I have a generator."

She nods and bites her lip. "I figured I'd just buy some extra groceries and hope for the best, but sure, yes, it would be amazing if we could come here. Thank you."

"Of course. And we can talk more later, but for now, Mands and I really need to game-plan." I know I'm being gruff, but every second standing around feels like lost time.

"Wait, that's why I'm here, actually. I've been following the forecast. I want to document you all in this storm. People need to see the hard stuff too. I don't know if they get how precarious this all is. Plus, uncertainty captures their attention."

"Captures their attention?"

"Yeah, people are gripped by not knowing what's going to happen—"

"So you want to turn what could be the worst event in the history of this farm into . . . engagement?"

"No, no." I watch Paige's features fall as she realizes we're having very different reads of her idea. "I didn't mean that. I just meant that people *care* about Two Peas. And the more people who do—the more people who are invested in watching what unfolds—the bigger your audience. Your community."

I take a deep breath. "Paige, unless this 'community'"—I use air quotes around that word—"can come and bulk harvest and move tools to high ground and dig ditches to help improve our chances of drainage, I don't really see why I should be caring about them right now."

"Frankie," she sighs, gently, like she's frustrated with me too. "I don't think you understand the support this could lead to. No matter what happens with the storm, your online community will rally. We could fundraise, sell T-shirts if we need to."

I am starting to feel my temperature rise. It's defensiveness and frustration bubbling through me. I am not in the mood for new ideas right now, especially from someone whose idea of action involves a phone, not a shovel.

"She has a point," Mands says. I didn't even realize they were listening.

My patience is worn through. I take a deep breath. Part of me wants to kick them both out of my house so I can just deal with all of it by myself without having it be documented or even discussed. But it's obvious they both think this is a good idea, which probably means I need to at least consider it.

"OK, Paige, can you be a fly on the wall?"

"Absolutely. You won't even know I'm here."

The next few days go by in a frantic blur of managing volunteers and thinking through every possible worst-case scenario. Between me and Mands, we call in help from friends around town. I have one set of people armed with shovels digging ditches around the buildings and another cutting small cabbages and piling them into huge crates. I know if the storm wasn't coming and we could let them grow, they'd get so much bigger, but it's not worth losing them all. After the cabbages, that group moves on to getting the rest of the zucchini and all of the hot peppers.

Abby, who has been coming in right after she serves lunch at camp, is managing crop storage. She helps figure out the jigsaw puzzle of getting everything labeled and loaded in our coolers. Another group works on moving everything out of the shed and up to the old garage behind my house, which is way less likely to flood. Finally, we park the tractor up by my house too.

If it weren't all so nerve-racking, it would be fun, as if we were setting up for a big party or a wedding or something. But it's not fun. I vacillate between worrying the weather will be just as bad as they say and worrying it will end up not being so bad and we'll have spent all this time and energy picking things before they're ready. What if we're not doing enough? But also: What if we're doing too much?

The entire time, Paige follows everyone around and takes photos. Each time I catch her out of the corner of my eye, she's jotting down something in a small notebook that she keeps tucking in her back pocket. "Christiane Amanpour vibes," Mands says when they catch me watching her.

At the end of the day on Thursday, we've done everything we can. The storm is supposed to roll in later this evening and peak early tomorrow morning. I thank everyone and send them home. Abby gives me a big hug on her way to her car.

"Are you sure you don't want to stay here?" I ask her. I don't know where she'd sleep, but I'd figure it out.

"No, I'll be just fine. And I know you have a full house." She winks.

Paige has gone to get Bobby, so I do one final walk around the structures on the farm. I rearrange the sandbags we piled in front of the greenhouse door just to make sure they're as secure as can be. I double-check the ditches and consider digging them even deeper, but it's getting dark and windy out. I notice a few battery chargers that were left in the shed, so I carry them back with me to my house so that they don't get rendered useless if the structure floods.

I must've taken longer than I realized because when I walk through my front door, I am immediately hit with the smell of roasted tomatoes, the air thick with sweetness and a little garlic too. I go into my kitchen and see Paige transferring tomatoes from a sheet pan to a blender. Bobby is spreading mayonnaise on bread. "We brought the food we had at our house because I assume the power will go out and there's not a generator there. And I took some of the bruised tomatoes from the staff bin to make soup. Bobby is getting everything ready for grilled cheese sandwiches."

"Hi, Frankie!" Bobby says gleefully, seemingly unaware of how threatening the weather is and how exhausted I am. "Look what Fran can do!" Fran is sitting on the ground next to Bobby quietly, and apparently her trick is enjoying every bit of bread he keeps "accidentally" dropping to her.

"It smells amazing." I feel tears well behind my eyes. I'm sure it's just because I'm bone-tired that my emotions are on the surface, but the warmth coming from the stove overwhelms me. It's been years since I walked into my house and someone else was already inside, let alone someone making a meal. When my dad was alive, I did most of the cooking. Having Paige and Bobby in my kitchen, filling it with soup and laughter, feels like seeing a version of my life I've never even given myself the permission to imagine.

We eat dinner together, the three of us, and Bobby keeps me distracted with a story I can't quite follow about an obstacle course he helped build at camp.

After we eat, I pace the kitchen.

As we wash and dry the dishes, I hear the rain beginning to thrash against the windows. After a particularly loud gust of wind, a branch hits the side of the house. My eyes go wide.

Paige attempts to reassure me. "It's all going to be OK."

"You don't know that," I snap back at her.

"You're right, I don't know that. But I do know you did everything you could." Her voice is steady, like she's not judging me for my inability to contain my anxiety. *What a good mom*, I think to myself.

"Sorry, I'm just on edge. And I keep thinking about how much I regret not taking Mands's suggestions more seriously back when we had more time to prepare for something like this. I wish I could press rewind."

"Pivot!" Bobby yells, startling me. He's in the corner of the kitchen petting Fran. I forgot he was even there.

Paige laughs.

"What's so funny?" I ask.

Paige turns to me. "I've told him that when something doesn't go as expected or when you wish you did something differently, you just need to pivot. It's like PR 101. And also a good way to stop ruminating. Pivot."

"Pivot," I say, to hear the word aloud again. Just verbalizing it helps me move my feelings in a different direction.

"When you pivot, you're not giving up or walking away." Paige wipes down the counter as she continues. "You still have one foot in the same spot, you know? You're just turning. Trying a different perspective. Anyway, you know what I mean."

"I think I do."

Bobby starts singing a song that he's improvising on the spot. "Pivot, pivot, divet-y doooo, I love you!"

I smile at Bobby. "How do you feel about ice cream?"

He gives me two enthusiastic thumbs-up. "If I had more than two of these, I'd put them all up!"

I laugh. I find his hokiness endearing. Relatable. I take out three bowls, spoons, and a container of Lakeside Cones chocolate ice cream.

"Start scooping," I tell Paige. "I'm going to make my special topping."

"What's in it?" Bobby asks.

"Grab that olive oil over there," I tell him, gesturing.

"Olive oil?"

"Trust me."

"Okaaay, Frankie." Bobby is skeptical, but he brings me the bottle as I place a tiny saucepan of water on the stove and put a metal bowl on top of it. I add a handful of chocolate chips, and once they melt, I add a spoonful of olive oil and mix it all together. I drizzle our bowls of ice cream with the chocolate sauce. Bobby watches the whole thing in awe.

He takes a bite. "This is so good! It's kind of like that shell stuff but also like fudge?"

"Exactly. My dad taught me how to make it."

We eat our dessert in a contented quiet.

Bobby looks up from his bowl. "My mom and I are here without my dad, but I do have one."

Paige's eyes grow wide.

"Yes, your mom mentioned that to me. I actually only had a dad for most of my life, not a mom."

"Did she die?"

Sometimes I forget how direct kids are. But I also wish we were all more like that.

"No, no." I am not quite sure what, or how much, to say. I take a breath. "I think the best way to describe my mom is that she wanted to be a lot of things, but being a mom wasn't at the top of the list."

"I think my dad might be a little like that."

Paige seems shocked, and Bobby turns to look at her. "But my mom is the best mom ever." Almost instantly, Paige's eyes look glassy.

I grin. "Yeah, I think she's pretty great too."

"Can I have another scoop of ice cream?" Bobby walks his bowl over to me, oblivious to the weight of what he just said.

"At my house, the answer to that question is always yes."

An hour later, Paige puts Bobby to bed, and I sit on the couch in the living room with Fran. The rain has become an incessant pounding. The wind's whistling is so loud, you could mistake it for a train.

I close my eyes, tilt my head back, and scan my mental list of all the preparations we made and what our various responses will be depending on the severity of the damage. I don't even hear Paige come into the room.

"Hey, how are you holding up?" She picks a strand of Fran fur off my shirt. "I know preparing for it is one thing, but living through it is another."

"It's nice having you guys here. I didn't think about how it would feel to get through this night by myself."

"I'm really glad you invited us to stay."

"Hold on." I get up, leaving Paige with Fran to grab two glasses, some ice, and my dad's oldest bottle of bourbon, which I only dip into during emergencies.

I pour us each a finger, and Paige and I sit on the couch and nurse our drinks. She puts her hand on my thigh.

"I can't. Not tonight." I am spent, physically and emotionally.

She chuckles and slaps my leg gently. "I wasn't trying to get into your pants. I just want to be close to you."

I lean toward her.

I am not used to touch if it's not part of sex.

I rest my head against her shoulder. "I think Two Peas will get through this storm, but I don't think I can go through another. Not that I can control the weather."

I lift my head and hold it in my hands. She shifts to better face me.

"I guess what I'm trying to say is that I can't have the entire farm, my entire business, on the line like this again.

This is too hard." I start to cry, little tears making their way down my cheeks. The past few days of preparation have felt like pressure building inside of my chest, and this is a release valve.

Paige reaches for my hand and squeezes it. "What do you need right now? Do you want to talk? Do you want to just sit here together? Do you want me to leave you alone?"

"Can I tell you an idea, and will you tell me if it's too much?"

"Sure."

"I was looking at the coolers full of so much produce today, and there's no way we can sell it all at the markets this weekend. And that's if the markets even happen, depending on the weather."

Paige nods.

"And a lot of it will keep for a while, but we really don't have the storage space. So what do we do with it all? How do we not lose it entirely? And as I'm racking my brain trying to think of restaurants and other places I could try to sell to, I realized there might be an answer right in front of me."

Paige looks at me as if I'm telling a gripping story. "So?"

"Abby. I think Abby is the answer."

"I mean, yes, we love Abby. But how is she the answer?"

"What if I hire her to turn all of this excess stuff into soups or something that we can sell at the market? She could use the school kitchen in the afternoons. And maybe we can see how it goes and, like, I don't know, maybe turn that into part of the regular business."

"It's a great pivot," she says, and we both grin at each other like fools.

I let go of her hand, turn, and cross my legs so I can better face her. I feel excited by how she's looking at me. I want to tell her more. "OK, so, if money was not an issue, my real dream would be that we could build a small commercial kitchen up on the hill behind my house and Abby could run it. Two Peas could grow for the kitchen, and Abby could make all sorts of stuff we could sell in addition to the raw vegetables themselves. And ideally for every container we sell, we could put a container in a free fridge at the elementary school so that teachers and parents and just whoever needs something, they could just take it."

"This sounds incredible. But if it's about growing your business . . . does it make sense to give anything away?"

"Well, serving this community is my business."

"Ah, yes, I'm getting it. So it would be like a Robin Hood thing. Charge your market customers a lot for the prepared food so that you can give some away to people who can't pay those prices."

"Exactly."

Paige nods approvingly. "I love it. Can't wait to overpay."

I laugh.

"Did you just come up with this?" she asks.

"Yes and no. I've been thinking about something along these lines for a while, but the storm really kicked it into gear."

And sitting here with her—her hand holding mine, our bourbon glasses getting slippery with condensation—I sense the fence around my heart starting to open. Even though the storm is raging, I feel hopeful.

"I just don't want to let my dad down." My tears start to well again. I'm surprising even myself with my candor.

"Oh, Frankie." Paige squeezes my hand harder. "I obviously never knew your dad, but imagine him being anything other than proud. Impossible! You've kept Two Peas going. Everyone loves this farm and is eager to support it. Look how many people showed up to help. Everyone loves *you*."

"I just always wanted to keep everything exactly as he had it. Like if I don't change anything about Two Peas, maybe he's still here?"

"I don't know, sometimes the way to keep something alive is to allow it to change."

I grip her hand. "Will you sleep in my bed with me? And I mean just sleep." I fake a stern look.

"I would love that. But I will sneak out before Bobby wakes up. I don't want to confuse him."

"Of course."

I toss and turn all night. I flinch at each *bang* I hear outside, but strangely I also feel excitement blossoming in me. I'm starting to see a way for Two Peas to weather not just this storm but all sorts of ups and downs.

It doesn't hurt that this beautiful woman is asleep next to me. I watch her chest rise and fall with each breath. She is on her side, facing me. She's snoring softly. She's wearing one of my T-shirts. Around dawn, as if she can sense she's being watched, one of her eyes opens just barely.

"Hey," she says.

"Hey."

"I should go check on Bobby."

"I like having you in my bed."

"I really like being in your bed." She kisses my shoulder before she leaves the room.

XIII

PAIGE

Our boots squelch as we walk. All the southern fields—where the cabbages, peppers, and more were—are completely flooded. It's a good thing we picked them all. Rows and rows of collards and kale are submerged in water. It's a muddy, sad soup. I don't know what to say to Frankie, so I just walk with her as she takes it all in. My phone rings. It's Mands looking for Frankie.

I pass Frankie my phone, and she winces. "I'm only going to say this once, so enjoy it: You were right. We should've better prepared the farm ages ago."

Frankie hangs up and hands my phone back to me. She keeps walking, and I watch her for a moment. She seems so much calmer than in the past few days. There's no more anticipation or uncertainty. The storm hit. It did what it did. She walks with a confidence, a knowing that this is a low, but from here it can only go up.

I start scrolling the Two Peas account. Our following has skyrocketed in the last few days, with people tracking the weather from across the country and leaving comments like "I didn't know I could care this much about a vegetable farm" and "Please let the weather gods protect queer farmers!"

While I have nothing to do with running this farm, it feels rewarding to have helped build this audience, this community of people who care about it. Normally I measure the success of my work in book sales and buzz, in spreadsheets that chart mentions and reviews and tags. But seeing people care about Frankie and the team and the crops that she's responsible for is a type of satisfaction I've never felt from work. It doesn't feel like business. It feels personal. Meaningful.

And then I see one private message that seems a little dubious.

Hey, Two Peas team, my name is Joey, and I scout for the J. Davis prize every year. I'd like to talk to you.

Joey's profile is private, so I can't get more information on him. And the J. Davis? It's a $200,000 prize that's given to people doing, like, oncology research and gene therapy. I know it from my work with authors who are scientists and researchers.

I run down the field to catch up to Frankie, but it proves hard, since everything is so wet and slippery. I'm also tripping over my excitement to show her the message.

"Are you OK with me talking to him?"

"I mean, I don't trust some random guy on the internet who's promising two hundred grand, but what do I know? Just don't give him my Social Security number." She turns around to continue assessing the storm's damage.

Within an hour, Joey and I are on the phone, and his interest seems authentic.

"Listen, we've never given a prize in the agricultural sector, and as the grandson of a farmer, it's always bothered me," he explains. "I've been riveted watching your account over these last couple of days and thought Two Peas should be in the running—it'd send a strong message about the importance of small-scale farming and queer-led businesses. Anyway, I wanted to first connect and see if this sounded like something you'd be interested in applying for."

"Um, yes, absolutely." I know it's not a question for *me* to answer, but I can't help it. Who would turn this down?

He explains the invitation-only application process and then clears his throat. "There is one catch: We need it back in a week. Most applicants have already turned theirs in, but your account only just caught my eye. I was hoping to get you in before the official deadline."

"It's OK! Just very grateful to be noticed and invited." I can't help but perform chipperness, even as I turn over how Frankie is going to respond to the short notice. "We'll get it to you in a week, no problem."

In between bites of what I am convinced is the best sandwich I've ever had, I tell Frankie and Mands about the call and the deadline. We're sitting around the picnic table eating the lunch that Abby dropped off when she came to check on the farm this morning. There's thinly sliced ham, pickled carrots, sprigs of fresh cilantro, and something else I can't put my finger on.

Frankie is skeptical. "But there's no way we could actually get this prize?"

There's a question in her voice, like she wants my perspective and not just my blind enthusiasm. "I think you've got a shot. And I'll help you as much as I can. The application is simple. Surprisingly so. You just have to explain what you are currently doing and how the prize could help you expand to serve more people. And you need a few references, which I think would be so easy for you to get. I could help you write it all up if you want. I do this kind of thing all of the time—it's not that different from a press release." I take another bite. "This sandwich—why is this so good?"

"Oh, Abby mixes chili paste and lime into the mayo." Frankie is nonchalant, as if these are lengths everyone goes to for a midday meal.

"So." I rest my elbows on the table, trying to read Frankie. "What do you say?"

Mands looks at Frankie expectantly.

Frankie keeps her eyes on her lunch. "It all sounds amazing, it really does, but I bet a million people apply to this thing, and I just don't know that we would get it. I don't want to get my hopes up."

"I don't know if you will get it either, honestly. But I do know it'll never happen if you don't apply. What's the harm in trying? And remember: You can only apply if you're invited to apply. You are being invited."

"I don't know."

"Sleep on it. And if you're interested in going for it, I'll help with every step. This is right up my alley."

For dinner that night, Bobby and I sit on the couch in our cottage eating grapes, carrot sticks, cheese, and crackers while we watch *Babe*. I just don't have the energy to cook after all the adrenaline of the last few days.

My phone rings. It's Eve. I'm halfway upstairs to lie in bed to talk to her when she asks, "How are you feeling about him coming?"

With all of the stress of the storm and the excitement of everything happening online, I've almost forgotten that Jared is visiting this weekend. Though I would be happy to go all summer without seeing him, we did agree he'd come midway through to see Bobby.

"I feel nervous." I flop onto my mattress. "I didn't expect to find such a fresh start here so quickly, such an actual sense of community. And I don't want Bobby to never see his dad, but I am worried that Jared visiting will burst this bubble."

"See, if it were me, I'd change my number and cut him off entirely."

"Frankie's mom left her when she was just a baby." Telling Eve, I realize how I've latched onto that fact. "I'm just . . . seeing what it's like to have a parent disappear from your life and what a scar that leaves. I don't want that for Bobby."

Eve's tone instantly becomes gentle. "I get that."

"I am happy he hasn't taken this summer as a chance to disappear from Bobby's life. I sort of thought, maybe even hoped, he would. The wiser part of me is glad he wants to see Bobby, but it's also just been so much easier without him around."

"What's been easier? Things with Bobby? Or *other* things?"

I avoid the fact that she's clearly asking about Frankie. "Both, but things with Bobby . . ." I trail off, putting my thoughts together. "He's only just gotten settled in his new routine here, and I don't want Jared coming around to stir things up too much. Because then I'll be left with whatever he leaves in his path."

"Look, you know Jared's expertise is not creating stability for Bobby. He will show up with a thousand gifts and just as many empty promises. So why don't you just stick to your routine and weave him into it? His visit will change the temperature, sure, but it doesn't have to change your plans."

I nod and bite my lip. It's good advice, but I cringe when I picture it. "We start each Saturday at the farmers' market." Just like we did on the very first day when we got to Sungold. "I'm not sure introducing Jared to Frankie is a good idea."

"OK, I know you two haven't officially 'defined' anything yet, but it's obvious you and Frankie are in some kind of relationship. She and Jared will have to meet at some point, right?"

"It's obvious?"

"Paige . . . it's very obvious. You're with her most of the time when I call, and you always bring her up if you're not with her."

Yes, Frankie and I have seen each other nearly every single day. Yes, I feel a magnetic pull toward her body when I'm near her. Yes, I see a bright, fulfilling future for her farm and want to help her achieve it. Yes, I care about her, and I feel her care for me in the way she touches me and talks to me. I feel how she cares in general when I see the way she is with Abby, and the way she is with Bobby, and with her whole crew, and of course, with Fran.

"Just think about it—about introducing Frankie and Jared. But also, you don't *have* to go to the market if you don't feel like you're ready to cross that bridge."

"I think I might love her." I blurt it out. My muscles tense like I'm scared to move. Did I really just say that? Aloud?

I can hear Eve smile on the other side of the phone even though I can't see her. "I know you do."

"I was not expecting this, Eve. I don't know what to do with this feeling."

"Hell, enjoy it! Obviously!"

"But what would our life even look like together? Sure, I love being with Frankie, but could I actually live here in Sungold? Could Bobby? What would I even do? Things with Jared feel totally hollow, but they're also stable and predictable."

"Paige, I don't often pull the big sister card, but: You only live once. Do you want life to feel hollow?"

"Of course not."

"And how do you feel when you're with Frankie?"

The answer is so simple.

"Full. Absolutely full of life."

"That's all you need to know."

I'm still upstairs, processing my conversation with Eve, when I hear a knock on the door. Bobby gets to it before me. "Mom, Frankie's here!" Seeing her at my doorstep right after that phone call confirms everything I said to Eve. *It's her*, I think. *It's her.*

I walk down the stairs and hug her tightly. I don't want to let go, but she pulls back, completely unaware of the revelation I'm currently having. "I don't need to sleep on it," Frankie says. "I want to apply for the prize. And of course I'd like your help on the application, but I'd like to write the first draft myself. I think it'd be a good chance to reflect on stuff. But can I show it to you when I'm done?"

"Of course." I squeeze her arms, absolutely buzzing. "I'm here for you."

She smiles and nods. She gives me a hug and waves goodbye to Bobby, then grabs the carabiner holding her car keys and turns to leave.

I touch her elbow. "Wait, let me get my shoes."

I walk her out to her truck. The night air is humid and buggy. I don't care. I want a moment alone with her. I push her against the tailgate and kiss her.

"I want you so much," I whisper in her ear.

She grins. "We've got time." She winks. "I want to go write everything down before I lose my energy."

"Go."

As she pulls away, I realize she could've just called to tell me she was going to apply. But she wanted to come here and tell me in person. She wanted to see me. Maybe she also feels what I do whenever I'm with her: that I need her to touch me so I can make sure it's not all a dream.

XIV

FRANKIE

Paige let me know Jared was coming to visit Bobby and she was planning to bring him with them to the market. She said something about "ripping off the bandage" and asked if I wanted to talk more about it, but honestly I've been so distracted with the farm and the grant application that I said everything was cool and there was nothing to talk about and brushed the whole thing under the proverbial rug. He sounds like such a dud anyway.

But even with the heads-up, seeing Jared approach the Two Peas booth with Paige and Bobby feels like a punch to the gut. Strolling up to the stand, they look like a model family from a J.Crew catalog. She's told me about what he is like, but I didn't know what he actually looked like. I didn't know that he comes with a strong jaw and dark, thick hair like some Bradley Cooper knockoff. Worse, Paige seems like she goes with him. Like she's the paper doll cutout that matches his. I look at them and see something whole and complete. What I absolutely don't see is where I fit into any of it.

But before I can lose myself in any additional anxiety,

Bobby, sweet Bobby, lets go of Paige's hand, runs past the customers in line, and comes behind the table to give me a big hug.

"My dad is here, and he got me a new tennis racket!"

Of course he did, I think. "I didn't know you played tennis."

"I don't. But now I can!" When Paige and Jared step up to the table, Paige clears her throat. "Jared, this is my friend Frankie. Frankie, this is Jared."

Friend.

Jared reaches out his hand, and I give it a firm shake. So firm that he pulls his hand back.

I see Paige suppressing a laugh.

"Glad you are getting a chance to see the market, Jared." I can't bring myself to say it's nice to meet him when that would be a lie. Then I clear my throat and look past him. "I don't mean to be rude, but I have customers here I need to help."

Suzzanne, who's my number two today, emerges from the van, where she was organizing our overstock. She gives Bobby a high five and turns to me. "I can cover the booth for a bit if you want to take ten." Part of me wants to strangle her. I don't feel like hanging out with Paige and her goddamn *husband*. But I also haven't had anything to eat or drink since before I loaded the van this morning.

"Bobby, want to hang with me? You can help me refill the zucchini bins." Suzzanne is being generous, but I wish she wouldn't be. I was hoping Bobby would be a buffer.

Paige, Jared, and I walk over to Marisol's Tamales. We

all wait in line for Marisol's famously spicy guajillo and queso tamales. I'm distracting myself by pretending I can't decide which flavor of agua fresca to get.

There's awkward silence. Paige looks as uneasy as I've ever seen her, clearly unsure of what to say or do. I wish she would say something. *Do* something. But she's frozen, like a prey animal. So I take one for the team.

"Paige says you're in finance?" I ask Jared.

"Yeah, I was in private equity for years, but now I'm CFO of a friend's start-up. We went to business school together. Harvard."

"I've heard of it."

He smirks. "Where did you go to school?"

"I didn't go to college."

"Yeah, that makes sense. You don't need a degree to pick vegetables."

Paige nudges him with her elbow. "Jared, Frankie runs her own business and manages a big crew. She is like a CEO, a CFO, an HR department, the entire sales team, a tractor mechanic, and a greenhouse expert all in one."

I feel both flattered by Paige stepping in to defend me and annoyed by it. I'm not embarrassed I didn't go to college. I know I don't have anything to prove to this guy, and yet I also feel like I want to show him up. It's a confusing mix of emotions.

When it's our turn to order, Jared takes out a black metal credit card and hands it to Marisol, who refuses it, pointing to her "cash only" sign.

"Who even carries cash these days?" he asks. As if this

will convince Marisol to instantaneously accept his payment method.

"I've got it." I hand over a few bills. It's money I can't really afford to be spending, especially not on lunch for Jared, but I'd rather not make a scene in front of another vendor. Plus it feels kind of nice to shift the power dynamic here. Paige smiles at me, and I can't tell if she's trying to apologize or thank me, or if she just wishes we would all vanish into thin air.

We all take our food to a bench. I don't like the way it feels to watch Jared eat the tamale I paid for, but I'm so hungry that I put the emotion aside. Once he gets to the filling, Jared starts coughing. "Wow, this is so spicy."

I smirk.

He keeps coughing, really making a spectacle. He knocks his chest with his fist. "They need to put a warning on these things." There were literal signs at Marisol's stand, but I don't remind him.

Paige looks at me and shakes her head. Again, the meaning is murky. Is she embarrassed by him? I would be. Then again, I would never be in this situation—though I seem to, somehow, be in it. I finish my tamale and tell them I need to get back to my booth.

"We'll walk you there," Jared says and throws his mostly uneaten food in the trash. A total waste.

As we approach the Two Peas tent, he looks at the small group milling around and turns to me. I swear he puffs out his chest a bit. "It's weird." His voice is louder than it was before, as if he wants to make sure everyone can hear what he's about to say. "I've seen all the chatter about this farm online, so I thought the line would be much longer. Paige, you've really done a great job making it seem bigger than it is."

I see a few of my customers within hearing distance do a double take.

Is this guy just out to embarrass me? Has he figured out that Paige and I are sleeping together? Or is he just this big of a dick? I look at Paige.

"Jared! Jesus. Frankie is my friend."

"Your friend, huh?" he sneers.

I don't know what to make of his response, and before any of us can say anything, Bobby runs over and tugs on Jared's shirt and points to another booth. "Dad, can we get cider donuts?"

"You mean empty calories? I think we should get out of here and play some tennis. Get our bodies moving."

I cringe.

So does Paige. "We should probably get going and let you get back to work."

As they turn to leave, Jared reaches for Paige's hand. She takes it, probably out of habit, but then quickly drops it. She turns back to see if I'm still looking at her. If I caught that handhold.

I am looking at her. I did see it. And I feel like I want to throw up.

XV

PAIGE

After Bobby has gone to bed, I tell Jared we need to talk. He is sitting on the couch in my cottage. I pull up a chair across from him. I want to look him in the eyes when I say everything I'm about to say.

"The way you behaved at the market was completely unacceptable."

"What are you talking about?" He's scrolling absent-mindedly on his phone.

"The way you talked to Frankie and the way you talked about her farm. All of it. Including that completely unnecessary donut comment."

"Oh, come on. It's not like you'll see this person again once your little Sungold summer camp experiment comes to a close." He gets up to go into the kitchen.

"Sit back down. I'm not finished here." I never talk to him like this. But being in a space that has nothing to do with him makes me feel empowered. So does the fact that I'm not just trying to stick up for myself. I'm sticking up for Frankie. And for Bobby too. "Frankie is not just some *person*. She's my friend. She's important to me."

"I knew it! I fucking knew it."

"Knew what?" I feign dumb.

"Oh, come on, I've known you for almost twenty years. I know you. So is that what you're telling me? You're leaving me to come put on overalls in the country and milk cows with your girlfriend?"

"First of all, Two Peas is a vegetable farm, not a dairy farm. Second, I don't have a girlfriend." I know it's a chicken response, but it's technically the truth. Frankie and I haven't had that conversation. Yet.

"So when are you coming home? The summer is almost over. Are you just going to stay in this shitty house with no air-conditioning and piles of laundry?" He nods his head toward the baskets of clothes I haven't had time to put away.

"I do need to come back to the city earlier than I planned, but—"

"Great, you and Bobby can drive with me tomorrow, and I can send someone to pick up your stuff." He talks as if this whole place and my life here are completely disposable.

"Jared, let me finish. I need to come back earlier because I'm quitting my job. And I need to do that in person. I owe them that—"

"Oh, finally! I've been telling you to do that for years. We don't need the money, and it's better if you're home for Bobby anyway."

"Jesus!" I shout and then immediately lower my voice so that I don't wake Bobby. If he wasn't upstairs, I would scream. Jared has never seen me this incensed, and I know from how he's looking at me that he's taking me seriously. "Can you shut up for like five minutes? You're not letting me finish what I'm telling you here."

I take a breath. It's go time.

"I'm quitting my job not because I don't want to work but because I don't want to work *there* anymore. Because I want to live here, and I can't do that job here." I push my shoulders back and stand up even taller. "I'm burying the lede." I clear my throat. "Jared: I want a divorce." I say all of this in my strongest, steadiest voice. My work voice. My take-no-shit voice.

His jaw looks like it is about to hit the floor. "I thought you just wanted to get away for the summer? You want a *divorce*?"

I shake my head, both seething and exasperated. "I told you multiple times that I wanted this summer to be a trial separation. It hasn't been a vacation, like you seem to think. It's been a chance for me to see what life apart from you could look and feel like. And I hoped that it would be the same for you. A chance to reflect. But how you've spent your time is not my concern. What *is* my concern is taking this time to be here with Bobby, away from you and our house. To see what it's felt like, not just what I thought it might feel like. And sure, our life hasn't been a total walk in the park here, but I'm myself. More myself than I've been in years. I want to make a life here."

I let out a big breath.

I said it.

I did it.

"Fuck," he says loudly, sharply. I point up to urge him to lower his voice.

"What about our son? You want him to live here? Go to some crappy public school? Don't you want a bright future for him? He has so many more opportunities at home. You always say how important it is for him to be in a diverse environment."

"Have you ever even met any of his teachers? Helped him with reading? He doesn't need you mistaking a good education with keeping up appearances and being connected to the right people."

He can't deny any of what I just said, so he just changes the topic. "And what about you? Do you actually want to live here? There are no good restaurants. There's no theater. There aren't even sidewalks. You love living in the city. Come on, we have a nice life in Brooklyn. Just come home and we'll go back to couples therapy."

I laugh, actually laugh. It's a nice life on paper, and we've already logged plenty of hours in therapy. I sit up taller in my chair. "Be honest with me: Do you truly want to stay married? Are you happy?"

"Is anyone who's married actually *happy*?" he retorts.

"Yes."

"Name one person, one couple, you know who's married and happy."

"Eve and Brian. Sofia and Claire. Raj and his husband." I roll off a few more names, and quickly I realize that except for my sister and brother-in-law, I've named all queer couples.

Jared lifts his eyebrows at me.

I shake my head.

"Do any of them have kids? Name one happy married couple with kids."

"Jared, you know Eve and Brian's kids. They're your niece and nephew."

"Right."

"Also, this doesn't matter. Let me be really clear: *I* am not happy."

He covers his eyes with his hands and rubs his face in distress. "Me neither," he says into his palms.

I shift my tone so it's a degree warmer. "Jared, don't you want to be happy?"

"I guess you're right."

"I'm what?" I don't know if I've ever heard those words come out of his mouth.

"You're right. Neither of us is happy. I'm not ready to talk about the rest of it, but I'll concede that." He lets out the kind of big sigh that feels like a truce, and then we just sit there for a minute, staring at each other, mouths agape. Like a big cloud of uncertainty has lifted.

Then I get up from my seat to get him a blanket and a truly sad spare pillow so he can sleep on the couch.

For the past twenty minutes, ever since Jared left to take Bobby to camp before driving back to Brooklyn, I've been sitting on the couch nervously bouncing my leg up and down, phone in hand, staring at Frankie's name on the screen like it might rearrange itself into the answer I need. I keep running through all the ways this conversation could go, and none of them is good. My stomach is tight. I've rehearsed what I need to tell her a dozen times, but it all still sounds wrong in my head. *Just call her.*

I hit dial. The phone rings and rings, and I almost wimp out and hang up before her old-school answering machine kicks in. At the beep, I speak into the void. "Hey, it's me. I'm really sorry about the market—"

Frankie abruptly picks up. "Hi, sorry, I was in the shower."

"I'm really sorry about the market. That sucked."

"Yeah, it did."

"I probably shouldn't have brought Jared there. I really didn't think it through."

"Yeah," she says. No more than that. Just *Yeah.*

"Look, I need to tell you something."

Frankie doesn't say anything.

"Are you still there?"

"Yeah." She's being so quiet that I can practically feel how upset she is through the phone.

"I am going back to the city earlier than I planned—"

"So you're just leaving? You're going with *him?*" I can feel her hurt and anger through the phone. She can't even say his name.

"No! I mean, yes, I'm leaving, but I want to come back. I'm just going—"

Before I can finish, Frankie cuts me off. "I've decided not to apply for the prize."

"What? Please don't do that just because you're mad at me."

"Not everything revolves around you. I just can't get my hopes up about one more thing just for them to get shattered."

I feel her words in the pit of my stomach. "Listen, if you don't want to apply, that's your choice. But if this 'getting your hopes up' thing is about us . . ."

She sighs. "I don't know, Paige." Hearing my name said like this makes me feel like I'm in trouble at school. "I just think maybe we got too serious too quickly."

"I feel like we had no other option, like since the moment I met you, I couldn't *not* be near you." I am feeling desperate and like everything I'm saying isn't coming out the way I want it to. I'm frustrated. "Look, I know when I get excited about something, I have laser focus. It's what makes me good at my job, but sometimes it means I can go too hard. Maybe it was childish of me to get so attached so quickly. But Frankie, it wasn't just me, right? I feel like we both are so drawn to each other."

She doesn't answer. She doesn't say anything. The silence is painful.

"I told Jared I want a divorce."

"Am I supposed to be excited about that? That's what you've said all along."

"I know. But I hadn't told *him* that yet. In those exact words." I want her to take this as the good news it is.

But she just sighs again, more loudly. "I feel like everything was easier before you came around."

"Easier?"

"Yeah, less messy."

My frustration amplifies. Now I'm frustrated not just

with myself but also with Frankie. "I know I try to pretend it's not—or at least I used to—but life *is* messy."

"Look, I need to concentrate on Two Peas. Now that we got through that storm, I need to make sure we're better prepared for whatever's coming. I need to give it all my energy. It deserves that."

"And I can help you!" I exclaim. "The reason I'm going back to the city earlier than planned is to quit my job in person. I've decided I want to give life here a real go."

"Paige, please don't quit your job and move here for me. That's too much pressure."

"That's not what I'm doing." My neck gets hot. I'm feeling defensive.

"I think we just need a little space. Just to think about things. I'm not saying this is over, but I do need some time alone for a bit. To focus. And figure out what I'm feeling."

What I want to say is *No.* What I want to say is *But I love you.* What I want to say is *I'm moving for me, but can't you be a part of that too?*

"Sure," I tell her. "How much time?"

"I don't know, Paige."

"Will you let me know when you do?"

"I have to go," she says and hangs up, my unanswered question lingering in the air like smoke.

XVI

FRANKIE

"And he said it loud enough for everyone to hear!" I replay Jared's charming monologue to Abby, who is on my couch petting Fran.

I'm not sitting with them because I cannot stop pacing my living room. We had planned for her to come over so we could talk about her turning the excess Two Peas vegetables into prepared food, but so far, I've only vented. "I knew it. I knew relationships were not my thing. I've been happily single for all these years. I knew I never should've started anything with her. It's just all too messy. He's such a prick. You should see him. He looks so entitled." I'm all over the place, I know. But I just need to get it all out. "I should've never opened myself up to someone, especially someone who's never been in a relationship with a woman."

"To be fair, you haven't been in a real relationship with a woman either."

"Whose side are you on?"

"This isn't a basketball game."

I just stare at her.

"Frank, of course I'm on your side. You're my best

friend. You're my family. But I care about Paige, especially because I know she cares about you. Anyway, go on, you're on a roll."

I take a big breath, like I'm readying myself for another round. "She's just so demure around him. Like he's got some power over her or something. Maybe because he's rich? I don't know. A part of me gets it. I do. He can provide all sorts of things, like private school and new tennis rackets and roller skates. He could probably just pay for the rink itself if he wanted to. And then there was this whole totally fatphobic thing about a donut that he absolutely intended for me to hear—" I am exasperated.

Abby cuts me off before my laundry list of things to fume about grows. "What Jared said at the market was awful. Clearly. And it sucks that Paige didn't stand up for you or the farm more."

I just nod vigorously at this, as if to say "Duh."

"But I think Jared was probably intimidated by you."

"Intimidated by me?" I scoff. "How could he be intimidated by me? I don't think he was intimidated. I think he's just an asshole."

"Both things can be true. He's for sure an asshole. *And* I think he was trying to peacock because he's an insecure man intimidated by his soon-to-be-ex's new girlfriend."

"I'm not her girlfriend."

"*Frankie*. Anyway, just think about it for a second. She left him and took their kid with her. I would bet he's feeling some shame about all of it. And I'm assuming he's not so dumb that he can't see how she is around you. And the idea that she's got someone new in her life, and a woman at that—not that that matters, but it probably matters to him. Anyway, I think he was trying to make himself look big and important. He has a lot more to prove than you do."

"Well, she introduced me as her friend. But then he made some comment about it later that I didn't quite understand." I stop pacing and press my hands to the top of my head.

"It doesn't matter what he knows for sure. The way you two look at each other says it all. She lights up when she sees you. It's obvious. Yes, ideally she should've backed you up more. But she's in a really tough spot."

"A tough spot she put herself in." I breathe out a long sigh. "I'm just so mad at her. And I'm mad at myself for letting things get this close and serious between us." I let out another long sigh, this one more defeated than the last.

"What is it?"

"Jared wasn't wrong about the line. It wasn't that long today, which also freaked me out. Business is down. Even though people are rallying for us online, they aren't showing up in person the way I hoped they would. And now she's planted the seed for this big prize, and I want it so badly, and I just don't think there's any chance in hell we'll get it." I feel my tears starting to brim.

"Frankie." Abby reaches her hand out to me.

"I'm just so embarrassed."

"You have nothing to be ashamed of. You've kept Two Peas going for so long. It's not like your dad left it to you in such great shape, by the way. He kept track of sales on the back of a paper bag! He gave nearly all of his vegetables away for free to just about everyone. Bill was an amazing dad and a great farmer, but he was not a great businessman." Abby laughs, and there's so much love in it that I join her.

My dad was so generous, to a fault when it came to his finances. But I can't imagine wanting to change that about him?

"It wouldn't be the end of the world if the farm had to come to a close." Abby pats the cushion next to her, and I join her and Fran. "I know you don't want to hear that, but it's important that you know that. I know you never want to talk about it, but I've witnessed how hard it's been to keep it going. I see it. And if you couldn't do it anymore, that would be OK. You wouldn't be letting anyone down. And you wouldn't be alone. I would help you. And you know Paige would too."

My tears start to fall.

"You can cry. That's OK too."

And so I sit on the couch and sob. Abby puts her hand on my back and rubs small circles, and I just let it rip. I cry for how hard it's been to make the money work, and I cry for my farmers who would be so sad if I had to let them go. I cry for Mands and how persistently they've been trying to get me to see things clearly and how stubborn I've been about it. I cry for the times I've insisted we do things the old ways without even considering how some of the new ways might ease our struggles.

And I cry for how much I miss my dad. I cry for the little me who never understood why my mom left. I look at Fran and cry about her too, because she is so old and I know my time with her is finite. I cry until there's nothing left in me.

Abby slows the circles she's making on my back, then gives me a bear hug.

"I never let myself do that," I say into her shoulder.

"It's good to let it out. Can I say one more thing?"

I nod.

"You have every right to be angry about what happened at the market, but I think you're probably also a little scared."

"Scared? No, I'm mad. What would I be scared of?"

"Of being in love. Because you're falling for her. And letting Paige all the way in scares you. Because if you do, you could get hurt."

I neither agree nor disagree. I just sniff and nod.

Abby's tone becomes even more gentle. "Could the Frankie of just a month ago imagine how happy you've been with Paige? At least before what happened at the market?"

"What's your point?"

"That, yes, opening yourself up—to Paige, and to Bobby too—could mean getting hurt. But it could also mean being happier than you've ever been. Because lately you've seemed really happy. Like I haven't seen you since before Bill died. Opening yourself up could mean having support for your dreams of making the farm really work, and also support if it doesn't. But more than that—it could mean having two people to share your big, Bill-sized heart with."

I start crying more. Where are all of these tears coming from?

Abby lets me sit with all of this. "You deserve to be happy. And I think you're at a safe enough point in your life to give it a try—so why not give yourself over to it?

You know as well as anyone that life can be short. Why not give yourself the chance to experience being in love?"

"And if it all falls apart?" I wipe my face with my sleeve.

"Then we'll sit back on this couch, and you can cry about it with me. But Frankie." She looks me straight in the eyes. "My Spidey sense tells me that's not going to happen."

"But it's so complicated."

"What's worthwhile that isn't?"

I wipe my chin and my cheeks. I look at my kind, wise friend who seems on the verge of tears herself. I close my eyes and take in everything she's said. "I don't think I'm cut out for this."

She raises her brows. "That doesn't sound like something Bill's daughter would say."

XVII

PAIGE

It's been a few days since Jared left, and I haven't heard from Frankie. And as desperately as I've wanted to call her or stop by Two Peas, I've respected the boundary she asked for and stayed quiet. I'm giving her space. Space, it turns out, sucks. But it has given me time to prepare what I'm going to say to my boss. And to call a divorce lawyer.

I pull up to Sungold Elementary to pick Bobby up from camp before we go back to the city tomorrow. I'm early, and Abby is standing outside the door to the cafeteria's kitchen. She's checking over an order that's just been delivered. Do I say hi? Pretend I'm on a call? Before I can figure out my move, she walks right up to me. Is she going to yell at me? Berate me for upsetting her best friend?

She skips right over hellos. "I just want to tell you that when Frankie puts up a wall, she only knows how to make it out of brick."

"What does that mean?"

"Look, Frankie would kill me if she knew I was having this conversation with you, but I love her like family and I feel for you, and I don't think this thing between you two is over. I think the fact that it is so real scares the shit out of her."

I look down at my sneakers, much less white than when I arrived, then back up at her. "I just don't get why she would throw it all away after that one moment with Jared at the market. And I know that was terrible, but if that's all it took for her to throw in the towel . . ." I know I'm dumping too much on Frankie's best friend, of all people, but I can't seem to help myself.

Abby shakes her head. "I think Jared made her realize how much she cares about you and what you think of her. I think she just felt really small, and that made her spiral and talk herself out of being in a relationship. I think she's so scared of having her heart broken that she would prefer not to make it available at all. Plus, the stuff between you and Jared makes things complicated, you have to admit."

"It does. I know it does."

"Anyway, I think the fact that she submitted the application is a really good sign."

"Wait, she applied for the prize? She told me she wasn't going to."

"Yeah, that's what she told me too. And then yesterday, she said she handed it in. It's a real breakthrough for her, honestly—that she's willing to put herself out there, even if it's not a sure thing. I know she's still gathering her references, but I think it's pretty much all set."

I smile. Even if I don't get to see this through, I'm so pleased Frankie applied. That she took a chance on herself. That she believes in herself enough to try.

Abby opens the door to the kitchen and cocks her head. "Also, Frankie is more of an action person than a conversation person. I feel like to get her back, you need to show her how valuable you know she is. Not just tell her."

I stand there waiting for more.

Abby just laughs and steps inside. "I have faith you'll figure something out."

XVIII

FRANKIE

"Frankie, easy!" Mands is directing me as I operate the small excavator we rented. We are creating proper trenches around the greenhouse and the tunnels. The hand-dug ones helped us in the storm, but they aren't sufficient for what could come next time.

I keep hitting the ground too hard, too fast. Ever since Paige left three weeks ago, I haven't been able to focus the way I usually can. I'm distracted all the time and mopey too. I know I'm the one who asked for space. Who asked for time without saying how long. But I'm miserable.

I turn off the machine and tell Mands I need some air. They are kind enough not to point out that we are already outside.

I thought pulling back from Paige would just reveal that we got caught up in everything way too soon and way too fast. I thought a little distance would reveal that we were just acting like lovesick teenagers who couldn't keep our hands off each other. But what I've come to realize is that, yes, life is less complicated without Paige. But it's duller too. Sure, I miss kissing her and sleeping with her, but what I really miss is just being with her. Being in each other's lives. Being attached.

These weeks without her have been so quiet. Too quiet. I miss the noise she brings into my life. Asking us all a million questions while she points her phone around the farm. Laughing under the blare of '80s music as we watch Bobby do lap after lap at the rink while we double-dip french fries. Bombarding me with her constant ideas, her "Have you ever thought about . . . ?" and "Do you know what might be a good idea?" and "This might be a terrible thought, but . . ." I miss the way she figures out life out loud. I miss the way she sees change as opportunity. The way she came to Sungold and threw herself into everything here. Her belief in Two Peas, her confidence in me and Abby and what we can build together. She's so unafraid to think big and then go after it. Unafraid to pick up life by its shoulders and shake it hard enough to sift out whatever isn't working.

I miss the way I felt when I knocked on her door and when I heard her knock on mine. Those assured, resonant taps. That feeling of knowing the person I most wanted to be with was right there, just on the other side, and she couldn't wait to see me just as much as I couldn't wait to see her. I just . . . miss her.

Fran and I are both half-asleep on the couch after dinner when I hear a car door slam. I look through my window and have a hard time believing what I'm seeing.

It's Paige. She's here, as if I conjured her. I'm out in

my driveway without any shoes on before I've considered what I want to say to her or how I want to be around her.

"Is it OK that I am here? I know you asked for space, but you didn't say how much. And, well—" She's talking nervously, like she's been waiting to get the words out for days, for weeks.

"It's OK you're here," I say. I nod at her. I steady myself. "I'm happy you're here." And that simple admission is all it takes. We both reach out to hug each other at the same time. Seeing that I'm open to touching her, she pulls me closer, wrapping one arm around my back and another up to my shoulder. She holds on to me tightly, her grip revealing her tangible relief at being reunited. I hold her just as tightly, feeling the tension of how we parted dissolve like hot breath in cold air.

"Frankie, I'm so sorry." She speaks into my chest. Hearing my name from her mouth is a balm that calms my agita of these past few weeks. She pulls herself away from me slightly so that she can look at me. "I'm so sorry for not thinking through Jared's visit more and how it would affect you, how it would affect *us*, and also for pushing you too much *in general*. Two Peas, the prize, everything—I kept pressuring you without thinking about how it might feel to put yourself out there like that. I'm sorry that I get so excited about ideas that I forget to come up for air and ask you what you think and how you feel."

I'm hearing, and feeling, how much this has all been weighing on her. I can't help but smile at her flushed cheeks and wide eyes. How she's bringing as much urgency and conviction to her apology as she does everything. I press my lips against her forehead. Not so much a kiss as a point of connection. "I love how excited you get. How passionate you are. And I don't talk about my feelings very easily. It's not your job to pry them out of me."

She nods.

I realize as I tell her this that it's on me to express my emotions right now. To give them to her without her asking. "I didn't mean to not be in touch for so long. It's because I was scared. Not because I didn't care. But because I do care. A lot."

I look at her now and see that she already suspected this but didn't anticipate me telling her, and that urges me on. "I care so much about you. And Bobby too. And I haven't ever felt this way. I've kept my life small on purpose. I try to control as much as possible, hold all the things that matter to me closely, so then nothing will leave me. This is scary for me."

I feel myself starting to get teary, and I see that Paige is too. Fran lumbers out from the house, curious enough about the hubbub to leave her station on the couch, and presses her nose to Paige's leg. We both bend down to pet her.

I dab a knuckle under my eye. "But after I told you I wasn't going to apply for the prize, I got to thinking about how small I've kept things. And how you see the possibility for things to be not just bigger but also better. So I changed my mind. I applied."

She fights a smile, and I can tell this isn't news.

"You knew?"

"Abby told me." She laughs.

"Well, I'm sorry you didn't hear it from me. I know that had it not been for all your efforts, I never would've been invited to apply. And I'm sorry I didn't take you up on your offer for help. I just wanted to do it on my own."

"I get that." Paige starts to get a little squirmy.

"What?"

"I might've sent in a reference letter you didn't ask for."

"You *might* have?"

"I did. I just wanted to do something to show you what a difference you make in so many of our lives."

I want to be upset with her for doing this on her own initiative, but then I scan the concern on her face and the rumpled, definitely not ironed T-shirt she's wearing. "Can I read it?" I ask.

I expect her to scroll to a document on her phone, but she pulls a piece of folded paper out from her back pocket and hands it to me.

> Dear Joey and fellow members of the Selection Committee,
>
> My name is Paige Segal, and I have worked as a publicist for notable authors for nearly two decades. This means I know how to craft and manage reputations and work with people who are eager to toot their own horns. Frankie Poster is not my client. In fact, she is pretty much allergic to the idea of building herself up. Frankie does so much good for her community not because she wants recognition but because it's the only way she knows.

> Though I'm aware Frankie has already submitted her application detailing everything about her farm and her vision for how your prize could help grow the important work she does, I fear it might not give you the whole picture of who Frankie is and why she is the best candidate for J. Davis. As Frankie is much too humble, I wanted to show up, as someone who loves her, to toot my horn loudly for her, to tell you that she is a true caretaker, a queer mentor for so many. She is a stalwart neighbor who knows what her community needs. I think you should hear from some of her fellow Sungold residents as well.

What follows are glowing quotes from crew members praising my leadership, my commitment to my community, and the safe and welcoming environment I've created at Two Peas. Fellow market vendors and local business owners—Raj of Lakeside Cones, Maya of Yolko Ono, Sam of Sam's—all crediting me with strengthening Sungold, honoring my family's legacy, and making the whole town proud.

I wipe the tears from my eyes. "You got all of those people to be a part of this?"

Paige audibly exhales, visibly exasperated. "My god, Frankie, you do so much for everyone. They were all thrilled to be able to help you in some small way, even if it was just a quote in a letter. I don't always think you know what you mean to people. I don't think you really get how much you just being you makes so many people's lives better."

"I don't do anything anyone else wouldn't do."

"You don't have to underplay yourself. I love everything about you, except when you do that."

My brain hangs on to the word *love*. "About that. You said you had to write the letter *as someone who loves Frankie*."

She stares me in the eyes, like I couldn't be more dense.

"Of course I love you." She says it as if it's the most obvious thing in the world.

She reaches for my hands and takes them in hers. "I think I've loved you since I met you. It's not just the big things about who you are but also the little things." Her voice goes up an octave. "I love how much you love tomato sandwiches. I love how much you love *all* sandwiches. I love how your body moves like an elegant truck, like you're totally unstoppable, but you always look out for everyone around you. I love how much you love to be in the water naked, and I love how you make me feel when you kiss me. I love learning the story of every tattoo on your body. I love that you're a total Luddite. I love that you love roast chicken so much that you'll even make one in the middle of summer. I love the way you smell, like bug spray and dust and dirt and cucumbers and soap and drugstore shampoo. I love that you make your bed every morning, even when you get up before it's light out."

"Can I talk now?"

XIX

PAIGE

I promised myself that if I didn't hear from Frankie for a month, I'd drive up to Sungold. I barely made it three weeks.

And now, it's surreal to be sitting with her back in her living room, where we kissed for the first time and where we weathered the storm. She's poured us each the tiniest bit of her dad's bourbon, as if her getting her feelings out is its own kind of emergency.

She takes a sip to wet her lips and clears her throat. "Paige, I love you so much—"

Something fizzy shoots through me, but I keep quiet as she continues.

"And I've had time to think." Frankie looks at me like she wants to track every reaction. "And I appreciate you giving me that time. It helped me realize some things." She gets very quiet.

"Like what?"

"Like I've been happier than I can ever remember since I met you. Like I've spent my whole life following in my father's footsteps, and it's OK if I make some of my own. Like he wouldn't be disappointed if I did some things differently. I think he would actually love it and be proud. Like just because he was a lone ranger after my mom left doesn't mean I have to spend the rest of my life on my own. Like because being with you isn't just being with you. It's being with you and Bobby. And I love him too. I love being an adult in his life."

To all of this, I nod. Tearily. But I feel like there's more coming. I just hold her hand and wait for her to continue.

She laces my fingers in hers. "Paige, I want us to be realistic. I don't have the resources Jared has. I can't offer you that kind of life."

"I don't want any of it." When I say it, I know it to be true. "I've spent a lot of time thinking about it. I stayed married to him too long for Bobby's sake, not for my own." I take a deep breath. "But then I realized that wasn't serving Bobby either. The resources Jared has aren't the resources Bobby needs. He wants to send Bobby to boarding school so he can conform better. But I don't want Bobby to conform to anything but himself. I want Bobby to be raised by people who are loving and fulfilled. I want him to be around people who aren't sacrificing their happiness just to have a big house and a fancy school. Jesus, he's *eight*. I want him to be around people who care about not just themselves but also their community."

Frankie nods.

"And that community? It's here in Sungold, Frankie. It's in this place that's welcomed us so warmly. It's here, and hopefully, it's with you."

She grips my hand tighter.

"It's with everyone here, really. It's with you and Abby and your friendship that shows me we can choose our own family. It's with your crew and their camaraderie and the whole town that rallies around each other. It's with everyone who's waiting in line at the market and actually enjoying the wait because it means getting to catch up with neighbors."

"I've always thought it's a good place to call home."

"I've been thinking about that a lot. About what home feels like. And it's what I felt this summer."

"So you're really coming here? Like for good?"

"I need to be really clear. I am not moving to Sungold for you. I'm moving because I think it's the right decision. And not just for me but also for Bobby. I thought it might be when I chose to spend the last few months here. But I definitely didn't know what it could lead to. I didn't even know I could meet someone like you. Scratch that. Not someone like you. *Actually you.*"

She smiles. I melt a little more.

"And I'm not leaving Jared for you. I'm leaving Jared for *me.*"

She nods. "And what about his relationship with Bobby?"

Her question feels sweet and thoughtful. I'm glad she cares. "Jared will visit regularly but not stay with us. Bobby's used to not seeing him for long stretches anyway, since he travels all of the time for work. I'm not naive enough to think this won't be confusing for Bobby, but life's messy. He'll be OK."

We both take a breath. Fran rests her snout on my thigh, and I pet her ears to steady myself.

"And before you think I'm some U-Hauling cliché, I

am not asking to move into your house with Bobby," I say with a laugh. "My sister and her husband are going to help me cover the rent on the cottage for a few months while I get my feet on the ground. Eve wants to spend more time out of the city, so we're sharing the cost of the house so that she and Brian can visit us whenever they want with their kids. I see bunk beds in my future."

"I can't wait to meet them all."

"Eve is dying to meet you. *Dying*."

Frankie smiles. She reaches up to smooth my hair, and I lean into her touch. I'm tempted to crawl onto her lap and press my mouth against her cheeks and her neck and every part of her. But this conversation is important.

"And what about your career? Don't you have to be in the city to do what you do?"

"To do what I *did*, yes. But you've inspired me to go out on my own. I want to do my own work now—smaller, with a more meaningful impact."

"Like you've done for Two Peas." Frankie reaches into her back pocket, pulls out a new iPhone, and wiggles it at me. I laugh. "I decided to join the twenty-first century," she says.

"Wait . . . does this mean we can finally text each other?" I ask.

"Sure, if you don't mind a thousand typos."

"Well, then, I need your number."

I open a new contact tab, and Frankie flips her phone over to show me a small piece of paper taped to her phone case. She's written down her number so she doesn't forget it. It is just about the most endearing thing I've ever seen.

I save it under "Frankie (Girlfriend)" and turn my screen to show her.

"Is that OK?" I feel sheepish all of a sudden. And very young.

She shifts closer to me on the couch and cups her hands around my face. She stares straight into my eyes. "I love you so much, Paige."

"And I love you. I'm so *excited*, but also, you know, nervous." I soften into her hands, leaning more of my weight into them. It feels so good to be held by her.

"Does it help to know I am too?"

I nod. I squeeze her hand.

"Want to be nervous together?" she asks me.

I nod again.

She leans forward and closes the gap between us. We kiss slowly, tenderly. We kiss like we know we have the rest of our lives to kiss. The air feels sweet and promising.

She pulls back a little and looks almost startled with realization. And then she asks me the most loving question of all.

"Have you eaten?"

Dig even deeper: Read the book's epilogue to see what Paige and Frankie are cooking up next and find their favorite farm-to-kitchen-table recipes to try yourself. Just scan below or visit 831stories.com/downtoearth.

ACKNOWLEDGMENTS

Thank you to Erica and Claire and the whole team at 831 Stories for investing in women's joy, desire, and pleasure. What a dream to finally get to work together after all of these years.

Thank you to Georgia Clark, who offered invaluable insights and actual ideas for how to implement them (I feel like I got to go to romance novel grad school!). And major thank you to Meaghan O'Connell and Sanjana Basker for their close reads and encouraging notes.

Thank you to my spouse, Grace, for everything, including their encouragement to try new things and setting an example themselves in their work. Getting to write Frankie and Paige's love story made me appreciate ours even more.

Thank you to my best friend, Cleo, for helping me figure out what an actual plot could look like and for the title (still awaiting your invoice!).

Thanks to all my friends at Long Season Farm for equipping me with farming knowledge. And to be very clear:

No character in this book is based on anyone at LSF! And Sam, thank you for the farm fact-checking.

Thank you to Jasmine Guillory for getting me into reading romance. And thank you to Roxane Gay for showing us all what it looks like to be a writer who can work in multiple genres and for letting me know I can be one too.

ABOUT THE AUTHOR

JULIA TURSHEN is a *New York Times* bestselling cookbook author. She writes a twice-weekly newsletter, teaches online cooking classes, farms part time at Long Season Farm, and is a competitive powerlifter. *The Washington Post* called her latest cookbook, *What Goes with What*, "absolutely genius." Julia lives in the Hudson Valley with her spouse Grace and their many pets.

ALSO FROM 831 STORIES

Big Fan by Alexandra Romanoff

A high-profile scandal derailed Maya's DC career, and she's eager to fly under the radar—that is, until her former boy-band crush reaches out with a job offer.

Hardly Strangers by A.C. Robinson

One night with a rock star could upend Shera's best-laid plans, revealing how a chance encounter can rewrite a story—and change everything.

Comedic Timing by Upasna Barath

Naina is seeking a fresh start in NYC after breaking up with her girlfriend, but when she meets someone at a party, he's so offtype that her attraction to him fuels an identity crisis.

Set Piece by Lana Schwartz

When a breakout BBC star gets swarmed by fans during a night out, it's a no-nonsense bartender, CJ, who rescues him—and warms them both up for an after-hours hookup.

Square Waves by Alexandra Romanoff

The first spin-off in the *Big Fan* series, an enemies-to-lovers romance in which tabloid fodder mixes with a long-brewing rivalry as Cassidy contends with her high-school nemesis.

Exit Lane by Erika Veurink

A postcollege cross-country road trip sparks *something* between Marin and Teddy—though it's not quite clear what. Over the next eight years, they have fated encounters on multiple continents.

Grape Juice by Eliza Dumais

When Alice lands in France for a wine harvest, she's disenchanted with her life. But she soon finds something she's missing in the vineyard owner's nephew Henri, who's just as lost as she is.

Rooting Interest by Cat Disabato

When Felix gets pulled off her NFL beat to cover the WNBA, she doesn't expect to find herself so taken with the sport—or with one of its biggest stars, Natalie Czapski.

Found Time by Caroline Goldstein

Lili and Reid lock eyes after a 1993 Jeff Buckley show. Thirty years and a whole lifetime later, they cross paths once more. Can they finally make their way back to each other?

Major Gift by Tiffany Ezuma

Ndidi, the widow of a billionaire tech mogul, is determined to give her wealth away—and keep one secret from Geoffrey, the perceptive journalist tasked with telling her story.

831 STORIES BOOK CREDITS

So many people were involved in bringing this book to life. Many of their names are included here, but there would be no HEA without the passionate work of booksellers and librarians and the enthusiasm of readers. And as we all know, romance readers are the best readers.

831 Stories

Erica Cerulo, Madison Feller, Marie Joh, Catherine Krenzer, Claire Mazur, Elaine Orihuela, Angela Vang

Authors Equity

Andrea Bachofen, Rose Edwards, Carly Gorga, Sarah Christensen Fu, Becca Kadison, Deb Lewis, Maddy McGovern, Madeline McIntosh, Nina von Moltke, Diana Simmons, Erin Vandeveer, Don Weisberg, Craig Young

C47 Design

Phil Chang, Haneu Kang, Jamin Lee, Naomi Otsu, Sunny Park

Editing

Sanjana Basker, Georgia Clark, Meaghan O'Connell

Marketing, Events, and Publicity

Emma Benshoff, Zoë Gillespie, Tara Larsen, Ashleigh Magee, Kaitlin Phillips, Riley Vaske, Kristin White

Production

Sam Martin, Scribe Inc.

Keep reading for a taste of

Rooting Interest

by Cat Disabato

from 831 Stories

1

Stepping into the arena, I feel a familiar crackle. The air sizzles like it's charged with electricity, like in the moments before a thunderstorm breaks.

The final few minutes before a game begins is my favorite thing about sports. It doesn't matter if the setting is a barely groomed field in a hidden corner of a suburb or a brand-new, state-of-the-art, $200 million facility in a major city. The feeling is always the same: anticipation, suspense, but most of all, possibility. Any team could come out on top. Any player could have the night of their life. The goals are specific and simple: play well; win. Off the field it isn't so simple, but that hardly matters here. Nothing gets me down in these moments. No matter how far I've drifted off course.

I'm supposed to be on the familiar sidelines of an NFL practice field, developing a rapport with Los Angeles Cougars rookies and coaxing quotes out of the coaching staff. While the guys ready their bodies and their plays during training camp, I am supposed to be filing stories about the new football season for the *LA Chronicle*. Instead, that beat—*my* beat, the one I fought for through innumerable late nights and with ruthless competence—has been plucked out of my grasp, as if it'd never really been mine at all.

For reasons too painful to consider closely—namely, that I am the sports section's only queer female staff writer—my editor reassigned me to cover WNBA All-Star weekend in Phoenix. I'm here because of my repeated requests to write more features, my editor, David, insisted, but the features I'd been pitching him were about football. Imagine my surprise when the response to my pitch about the Cougars' offensive weaknesses was an assignment to cover Natalie Czapski, the star player for the Hollywood Lights, and her comeback after an ACL injury.

I've never written about basketball. I've hardly ever watched it. But now, a scant few hours after booking my travel and scrambling to make my flight, I am going to have to figure it out. Even if the ground beneath my feet feels no more solid than sand.

At least the energy in the PHX Arena is familiar, the excitement sparking the air, boosting my mood and calming my anxiety as I wind my way through the crowd. Fans who look like they've been following their team for decades mix with overstimulated kids, couples holding hands, and chattering groups of friends. All-Star weekend means people are decked out like the color spectrum: red for the Las Vegas Aces, seafoam for New York Liberty, and burgundy for the Lights. In my usual work outfit of a black button-down and black pants, I fade into the background, just as intended.

I try hard not to come off as anyone or anything in particular when I'm on the job. To ticket holders, the press badge around my neck means I'm someone official, and to players, I'm nothing outside of my game knowledge and the questions I ask them—more of a conduit than a person. It's something I learned from David, who was David Greenebaum, sportswriting legend, before he was my mentor and my first-name-basis boss. Now that I am unexpectedly in a position of having to win back a job that I thought was mine, following David's lead—playing by his rules—is more crucial than ever.

When I make my way to press row, I'm mildly surprised to discover that it's right behind the announcers' table, close enough that I'll probably hear their commentary. I find my assigned seat between a young Black guy, who gives me a tight smile with "no new friends" energy, and a white person with a dyed-pink mohawk and, helpfully, a "they/them" pronouns pin.

They look at my badge, then my face, then my badge again. "Wow, is the *LA Chronicle* finally covering the WNBA? Or is this just for Nat's comeback?"

The small placard in front of them identifies them as a freelancer, someone used to being batted around by whatever publication decides to say yes to a pitch. And they clearly know that covering women's sports is still seen as optional at most big outlets.

I know how to play this. I shrug and say, "I go wherever they tell me to go."

They stick out their hand. "Danny."

"Jennifer Felix," I say, shaking it. "But everybody calls me Felix."

As I busy myself plugging my computer into the power

strip taped to the table, Danny makes conversation. "It'll be good to have CZ back in the four spot."

It's like they're speaking in a foreign language that I studied in high school, some vocabulary familiar but the full extent of the meaning lost on me.

"Totally," I say.

"Or do you think she'd do better in the five?" Danny asks mildly.

"She's, um, I think she's got something to prove so she'll step up in any role." It's not like I've said anything wrong. The problem is, I haven't said anything at all. When sportswriters talk, we argue about minutiae and one-up each other with niche facts and hot takes. I can tell from Danny's raised eyebrow that they can see right through me, see how little I know.

"Oh, honey," Danny says, almost sympathetically, but with a vicious little edge. I wonder suddenly if they'd pitched a WNBA story to the *Chronicle*, gotten the feedback that there wasn't an audience, only now to see someone totally ignorant of the game plopped down next to them to cover it. "You're really fucked, aren't you." Not a question.

"I'm a fast learner," I say.

"You better be," they say, and pointedly turn back to their computer. Conversation over.

I'm rattled, and I know it shows. Determined to shake it off, I return to my setup, straighten my laptop, and shut down any application I don't need. Sports is a world full of rituals (or superstitions, to the nonbelievers); players have their lucky socks or listen to the same song before every tip-off. And I have mine. I close my eyes. I take deep breaths through my nose. I listen to the sounds of the crowd, note the scents in the arena. The voices aren't just energized; they're giddy, and much more high-pitched and femme than what I'm used to from NFL fans. I hear the squeak of rubber soles on the arena floor and heels on the stairs. I smell popcorn, ketchup, and Dove deodorant.

This cataloging is a practice I copied from David. He wrote a book called, simply, *Writing the Game*, which my father gave me for my sixteenth birthday. My copy is so dog-eared, underlined, and just generally run-through that it's falling apart at the binding. One of the lines I've committed to memory: "Attending a sports game as a fan is a five-pronged sensory experience, so writing about sports should be the same." One twisted bra strap digging into the skin of my shoulder is the last sensation I identify before opening my eyes. I slip my hand under my shirt and untwist it, making sure everything is in its right place. I'm as ready as I can be.

The announcer's voice booms, *"Welcome to All-Star weekend!"*

The screams of the crowd swell to a new crescendo as the announcer starts calling out the first few players, none of whose names I recognize. Cameras flash as the announcer rumbles, *"Back from a season-ending injury to show us what a Big can do in this competition, and representing the Hollywood Lights, it's CZ, Natalie Czapski!"*

In my rush to research three decades of WNBA history, I'd reduced Natalie to her component parts: her wingspan, her layup, the design of her Nike sneakers, the muscle she'd put on after her rookie year and the speed it gives her. In doing so, I somehow failed to understand what Natalie looked like as a whole. She glides onto the court, all long-limbed grace. Her blond hair is pulled into tight French braids. On the Jumbotron, I can see how the turquoise blue accents on the Lights' uniform bring out the richness in her pale eyes. And how her big, crooked smile, which stretches across her whole face, makes her seem a little cocky—but also kinetic enough to power the sun. The way the tip of her tongue pokes out slyly between her teeth makes something hum in my rib cage.

She flexes her right bicep and laughs when the crowd goes even wilder. There's no way for me to hear her, but I can read her lips as she screams at them—at us: "LET'S FUCKING GO." My stomach and chest pulse with little bursts of want. Fuck. In my rush to get ready for this new assignment, I'd somehow forgotten that the WNBA is filled with my exact type: pretty tomboys with bravado. I'm pummeled by the unprofessional thought *Natalie Czapski is hot!!* I *never* had this problem in the NFL.

I can't afford distractions right now, so I turn my attention back to my notes. Tonight's the skills competition, followed by the three-point shooting contest, and I watch the first three players blaze through the stations, writing down their times for their exercises (39.2 seconds, 45.1 seconds, and an unfortunate 55.6 seconds).

I log any game vernacular that isn't immediately familiar to me in a section of my doc called "Terms and Lingo." For the Cougars, I have meticulously organized research and notes and quotes, everything at my fingertips and ready for me to draw on in an instant when inspiration either strikes or lacks so much that I need to rely on previously accumulated information. My new file has a "Questions" section that is twice as long as the rest of the document, filled with inquiries that I'm sure are mind-numbingly basic to even casual fans. Things like "What does it mean to 'space the floor'?" and "Where did Natalie Czapski go to high school?"

As I type, fast without looking at the screen, I watch Natalie in her seat, her infectious smile only disappearing when her jaw drops in awe as a contestant lands a neat three-pointer. Scanning the crowd, I see I'm in good company: Natalie's getting attention from all over the arena, everyone from former teammates who playfully squeeze her shoulder as they pass to a brunette sitting courtside in a handmade "CZ DOES IT" T-shirt. She is a magnet, drawing in focus and metabolizing it into charm.

When it's her turn, she strips off her warm-up jacket, springs on the balls of her feet, and shakes out her elegantly muscular arms. At the whistle, she's off like a rocket. This is when my years of sportswriting—even about an entirely different game—pay off. Some highly trained sliver of my brain automatically translates what she's doing on the court into dynamic language. She bounces passes into a row of progressively smaller nets, hitting her mark on the first try for each. She races toward the basket, sets up at the initial shoot zone, and drops her ball cleanly through the net. As she sinks the next, I note the way her fingertips graze the ball and the flex of her calves as she jumps with her shot. She's stunning to watch.

Natalie finishes her run with an easy layup and plants her hands on her thighs, her chest heaving with deep breaths as the announcer's voice booms out her impressive time: *28.2 seconds*. From the vibe of the arena, I can tell that no matter how the rest of the night goes for Natalie Czapski, she's shown everyone that she is *so* back.

She wins the skills competition—it isn't even close—and I take note of reporters buzzing around me. "That footwork—never would have known anything had ever been wrong with her knee," a guy with a buzz cut says. She could've stopped there and relaxed into the loose, playful atmosphere of All-Star weekend, but instead she goes into the three-point contest radiating the determination of someone with something to prove.

A player named Ruthie Jones makes enough three-point shots that it feels like no one can beat her, so when Natalie starts shooting, the crowd is loud and yammering, not paying much attention. But Natalie is doing even better than Ruthie, making more baskets than she's missing. The whole mass of us goes holding-our-breath quiet, falling into that calm that swoops in during a big play when it feels like an errant shout could disrupt the equilibrium and throw a player off.

"No," someone behind me whispers in awe. "She literally can't do it."

I glance back at the fan, two rows above and wearing a Czapski jersey; the Lights' logo, a playful riff on the Hollywood Walk of Fame stars, is nearly glowing on her shirt. The fan is squeezing her friend's hand, eyes locked to the court and sparkling. "She can't, she can't, she can't," the woman chants, but she's breathless in anticipation, using the negative to invoke the opposite: *She can, she can, she can.*

Next to me, Danny murmurs their own writing out loud, a copyediting trick to catch errors. "No player has ever won both the skills competition and three-point contest in the same WNBA All-Star weekend."

Natalie isn't just doing well; she might be setting a record. My own fingers fly over the keyboard as my eyes stay glued on her. She grabs her last ball, bends her knees, and shoots. It arcs balletically and slips cleanly through the basket. Even I know enough about this sport to think the word *swish.* The reverent hush gives way to explosive cheers. Natalie Czapski has made history.

I feel a flutter in my chest, the way I do when an article goes viral, like maybe this is less of a demotion than I thought. I could write a great piece here, especially if I trust that my storytelling skills are just as valuable as being a ball-knower. My uncertainty gives way to a more familiar feeling: determination. There is a good story to tell about Natalie, and I'm going to figure out how to tell it.

As I flash my badge to the security guy at the door of the media room, I hope I'm radiating "Can you believe this night?" buzz and not anxious "I'm new here" energy, but the feelings are a little muddled.

Basketball might be uncharted for me, but the organized chaos of this presser—press conference—is not. I'm intimately acquainted with the symphony of scuttling PR women backed by the frenetic clack of fingers on keyboards, the chaotic disarray of tangled laptop chargers and extension cords, broadcast camera people setting up their gear elbow to elbow. My eyes bounce off the smattering of old white dudes—they are everywhere in sports media, as pervasive as crabgrass—and slow to scan the faces that make me feel an unexpected sense of belonging. Even though I don't recognize anyone in the room, there is a surprising sense of the familiar in the people around me: a woman with a taper fade haircut, someone holding a laptop with "Protect trans kids" stickers, and a guy in the corner with a fully beat face. I can picture these people out at the dyke nights I go to in LA—just not at my sports bars. But here they are, with barely suppressed excitement to cover what turned out to be a momentous athletic event.

I find my seat in the second row. I start my voice recording and hope it doesn't catch my audible intake of breath when Natalie is ushered into the room. She was alluring from across the court. From less than six feet away, she's spellbinding.

I pull up the gamer on my laptop screen, the recap article that I need to publish as soon as possible, and while I review my stats and check the spelling of players' names, the reporters around me start asking questions.

"Natalie, congratulations. How does it feel to make history tonight?"

Like most professional athletes, she's been media trained into oblivion, giving the kind of basic, boring responses that allow beat writers to file their pieces and her to avoid controversy. It's standard stuff, nothing really inspiring. Tracking the patterns in the questions themselves is more interesting. We are supposed to be celebrating, but after that first question, everyone seems to have already moved past the significance of the moment on to the future of her game, asking about the pressure she faces, soliciting comments on how much is riding on her. I imagine my fellow reporters typing phrases like "crushing weight," "grim intensity," "tall hill to climb." I've made it as far as I have in my career by pushing into a story as far as it will give, and I sense there's something else we aren't getting here, something to be gleaned from that ever-present smile.

Natalie's night wasn't about proving something in the wake of her injury, I'm realizing as I take her in. It was about the joy of playing the game. This is a narrative I can weave without knowing all that much about basketball; I just need a good quote from her to make the piece work.

"We have time for one more," the team publicist says, and my hand shoots in the air faster than anyone else's.

"There, on the left."

"Hi, Jennifer Felix, *LA Chronicle*," I respond, pushing aside the flicker of warmth pooling in my stomach when Natalie turns her attention to me. "You looked like you were having a lot of fun out there. Were you having fun?"

"Yeah, I was having a great time out there. Anytime I get to be on a basketball court and playing, I'm happy."

Anytime I get to be on a basketball court and playing, I'm happy. It's a good kicker. I nod. "Thank you!" I respond.

Natalie's smile drops, and with a jolt I realize she doesn't see what I'm after. And that the version of her that radiates brightness has a darker flip side, a stone wall that blocks out the light.

"That's it?" Her voice is teasing, but not breezy. There is a real bite in her tone. "That's your question? Did you really just ask me if I *enjoy* playing basketball?"

"I wanted to hear about how you felt on the court tonight," I answer uneasily, the warmth in my core replaced by a sinking feeling.

"Do you have a basketball question? Because I have some basketball things to talk about." She rests her elbows on the table and leans forward, homing in on me.

Watching this on playback, a casual observer probably wouldn't read anything into our exchange because of Natalie's careful tone. They wouldn't be able to see the way Natalie's eyes lock on mine and the fact that there's no give in them, no humor at all. Her stare is a razor-edged challenge, a test I know I'm going to fail. I can't ask a basketball question because it will reveal that I don't know what I'm talking about, but if I don't ask a basketball question . . . it will also reveal that I don't know what I'm talking about.

"That's it from me," I say, hoping she'll let it die.

She doesn't.

She leans back in her chair, folds her arms across her chest. "I haven't seen you before. Do you know the league?"

I want to tell her that watching her play made me more emotional—felt more visceral—than a sporting event has in years. But that's not something a journalist can say, so instead I give her four words that couldn't be more passionless: "I'm working on it."

Her eyes narrow. "Working on it," she parrots, pushing back her chair. "Well, thanks for trying, I guess. Good-night, everybody." Then she walks out of the room, never looking back. I watch her go, shock giving way to anxiety and then painful, red-hot embarrassment.